A MATCH TO DIE FOR

Ellen Frank Mathews

ISBN: 1511769793
ISBN 13: 9781511769792

CHAPTER 1

"BEWARE OF THE ILLUSION OF FAMILY."

-- The Matchmaker's Bible

The technical word for someone like Marvin was asshole.

He stood on the doorstep of my Playa del Rey townhouse with an expectant expression. "Aren't you going to invite me in, Chloe?" he said in his falsetto.

I forced a smile. "I'm just on my way out."

"How's my foxy blonde cousin?"

"More like a silver fox with a little bleach." I cupped my hand over my forehead, afraid of getting cataracts from the strong morning rays.

"I sure could use a cup of coffee, but I'll settle for a cold drink," Marvin said.

A loud plane took off overhead. How else could I afford to live in a beachside community if it wasn't next to a runway? I motioned Marvin inside, vowing to myself he had ten minutes to drink up before I gave him the boot. My four-legged child, a cockapoo named Sweet Pea, growled at him.

"When are you going to get some tranquilizers for that dog of yours?"

Marvin's idea of a pet was a dollar-fifteen goldfish.

"So you're here to diss my dog?"

"Not exactly." His beady eyes shifted into overdrive. "You know the thirty-five thousand your mother willed you?" He ran his fingers through his salt-and-pepper hair. "I need it back. Well, I don't need it, the estate does to pay the IRS."

"Is this some kind of joke?"

"I wish it were." He dusted the dandruff off his shoulders.

"But you were the one managing her affairs."

"How was I to know she neglected to file an income tax return for the last four years?"

Marvin took the California bar ten times before he passed it, yet Mother insisted on making him executor of her estate. Then again, she spent most of her seventy-eight years in denial. A stand-up comedian,

Leah Silverman went for the laughs, depending on others to pick up her pieces.

I followed him through the living and dining rooms--a blend of Pottery Barn, Thomasville, paintings and tchotchkes--to the kitchen, trying to process the implications of the situation.

He opened the refrigerator and peered inside. "Don't you ever eat anything beside nuts and berries?"

"Better than forty-seven BLTs with mayo."

Thanks to my middle-age metabolism, I lived in carb rehab most of the time.

Marvin helped himself to a Diet Coke, flipped open the lid and gazed out the window overlooking a construction site that symbolized more traffic for a city already in need of passports to cross Culver Boulevard.

"What does the accountant say?"

"Leave it to the IRS. They'll follow you to the grave and beyond." He leaned against the granite countertop, which was part of a kitchen upgrade I was still paying for.

"How much does the estate owe?"

He took a sip, shifting positions. "Thirty-four thousand, eight hundred." His voice cracked. "Including penalties."

"This is not good news for a person who just went into business for herself."

A burned-out social worker who viewed the world in terms of married people--those who were, those who weren't, those who were going to be but didn't know it yet--I'd quit my job with the county probation department and used my inheritance to set up shop as a matchmaker.

Marvin brightened. "There might be another way. Remember my friend Alex Grand?"

"The guy who thought my goldie was too ugly to mate with his."

He nodded. "When Alex decided to become Alexis last year--"

"I'm still counting the zeroes in thirty-five grand, and you're onto transsexuals?" I inched toward him catching a whiff of his metal Coke can.

Marvin drew his lips into a snide smile. "She looks great, I'm telling you."

I raised my palm like a crossing guard. "Oh, no. No, no, no. I think I know what's coming. My match-making service is for traditional people seeking--"

"She's got money, lots and lots of money."

"It would take a Warren Buffet."

"Thirty-five grand, plus fifteen for dog food."

"Are you nuts?"

"Consider it a little dowry."

"Why don't *you* ask her out?"

"Nice legs but too tall and hairy."

Although there was no lack of females interested in By Invitation Only, the limited supply of males curtailed its growth and kept it in the red during its first six months of operation.

"How about you helping out, kid?"

Marvin ventured, "If I hadn't lost a bundle in the futures..."

I should have known better. The only thing he ever gave me was the mumps.

"Will you at least talk to her?" he asked.

"What makes this so important to you?"

"She needs all the help she can get."

For a moment, I thought I detected a note of compassion in his voice.

"And there just might be a little finder's fee," he said with a nervous laugh.

"I thought so."

"If you don't appreciate my efforts...On second thought, after all those years working with parolees--"

"Don't tell me what I can do." I heard my voice crescendo.

"With your track record--what are you on, number six?"

"Leave my ex-husbands out of this."

Number one was a Scientologist who tried to set my ethical compass. Number two was a Buddhist who abandoned me for a mountaintop. Number three was a Catholic who delivered more guilt trips than my

Jewish mother. After three marriages and a string of relationships, I was content to live alone with my dog Sweet Pea and leave the romance to my clients.

A smug expression flashed across Marvin's face. "So is it a deal?"

"What gave you that idea? Since the time of lollipops I've been matching dolls, dogs and people. When I finally decide to make some money at it, you come along and--"

"We're family," he reminded me. "I'd hate for the IRS to put a lien on your house." Marvin squashed his metal Coke can, tossed it in the trash and twisted the pull-tab around his finger like a wedding band.

If there was anything that infuriated me, it was feeling manipulated, and Marvin had done a good job of it. I fantasized about poisoning him with a batch of lily-of-the-valley brownies. I sped down Washington Boulevard on a March morning. The idea of taking on a transgendered person to pay off a debt was as preposterous as introducing my cousin to one of my clients. Life was tough enough without feeling trapped in the wrong body, and the commitment it must take to reassign one's gender was mind-boggling. How could Alexis be the same person as Alex? As a man she liked women but in her reinvented state favored men. What about her anatomy? How in the world did they make a vagina? Stop. I wasn't about to let curiosity, compassion or difficulty with the *no* word derail my life.

At Abbot Kinney Boulevard, I turned left and rolled into the lot behind my Spanish-style office building. I chose its Marina del Rey location to attract a clientele willing to pay ocean front prices for personal introductions. I parked and mounted the steps leading to my second-floor suite with the By Invitation Only Personal Introductions sign on the door.

A blast of heat greeted me in the lobby. I flipped on the air conditioning, threaded past the love seat and photo gallery of airbrushed smiling faces on the wall to my reception desk. I phoned my accountant, rattled off Mother's social security number and requested verification of her status with the IRS. Sure enough, Marvin was right: The estate owed the money. I couldn't decide whom I was more pissed at--Mother, the IRS, or my cousin.

While determined to find another way to pay up, I contacted Marvin and asked for Alexis' number. After all these years, what harm could there be in an innocent conversation?

Alexis answered in a voice that still evoked a five o'clock shadow and preponderance of testosterone. Sweet

Mother of Jesus. My marriages to the Scientologist, Buddhist and Catholic taught me to swear in different faiths.

"Are you still raising goldies?" Alexis asked.

"I've switched to cockapoos."

"I've switched a few things of my own."

"So I've heard."

"He's such a dear, that cousin of yours."

I made a face.

"I saw your ad in the paper. I've been meaning to call, and when Marvin told me--"

I lapsed into my spiel automatically. "If you're looking for a dating service, that's not what we are. By Invitation Only is a personalized introduction service for marriage-minded adults. Once we accept somebody, we offer three different packages."

"I'll need the giant economy size, honey."

I paused. "That'll cost you."

"How much?"

"Thirty-five thousand."

She sighed. "What I do for love..."

I cautioned her. "While I'm making no promises, if you'd like to come in and talk--"

"Does Pinkberry sell yogurt?"

CHAPTER 2
"RESIST ANYTHING BUT TEMPTATION."
-- The Matchmaker's Bible

Marvin was wrong. Alexis wasn't hairy, just tall. She marched into my office with a puppy mix in her arms. "Isn't he perfectly marvelous?" I swear Alexis cooed like a dove.

Despite her transformation, she had a long way to go to pass for the female gender. While her eyes were the same as Alex's, her brow line and jaw looked softer, and her lanky figure was starting to develop breasts. For a moment, I had the eerie sensation I was looking at a ghost of the likable nerd I came to know during my Berkeley days. Although he could be a bit aloof at times and prone to locker-room humor, I wanted him back and now.

She took a step closer to me, and I caught a whiff of cheap perfume apparently meant to extinguish any residue of her former self. I sneezed.

Alex the Great, or Alexis the Not So Hot, snorted a laugh. "Don't tell me you're allergic."

Facing downwind, I asked, "What's that fragrance?"

"Isn't it lovely?"

I sneezed again, overcome by its cloying nature. Of all the wildflowers in the garden of L. A., she was just another bit of eccentric flora and ought to seek out the services of another matchmaker with a less delicate nose.

As she zeroed in on the photo gallery hanging behind my desk, I recalled how Alex had been a bit arrogant, too, at least when it came to dogs. Her obvious wig did nothing for her. I would have suggested a new 'do, as well as a different fragrance, if I were going to take her on as a client, but the idea was ridiculous.

"How about this one?" She pointed to Paul.

"Too fat."

She indicated another.

"Too thin."

"What about him?"

"Too bald."

"I like bald men."

"Too short."

She plopped down on the love seat and crossed her legs like Alex. At least she believed in shaving them. Her slinky mini dress, bangle bracelets and stilettos emphasized a small-boned willowy frame. We exchanged the usual pleasantries.

Reluctant to lead her on, I said, "Just so you understand it's important for this to be right for both of us."

She tipped back her head. "Would you like me to leave?"

"Not yet." I felt disturbed at the possibility she had read my mind. "I assume you do more than rescue dogs these days."

"Oh, yes. At the moment, I'm working on a new generation of bomb." She had become Alex the scientist again, confusing me further.

I had a sudden idea. Maybe if I had gone out with him in college this never would have happened. He would be working today at Raytheon and living in El Segundo with a wife and two kids. On second thought, how presumptuous of me to fantasize about having such influence over another human being!

"What else would you like to know?" Without waiting for an answer, she said, "I was married for nine years and fathered a child, a son." She lowered her eyes to half-mast. "Whom I no longer see." Her voice caught.

While this wasn't the kind of information I wanted to hear from her, a wave of sadness undulated through me.

She uncrossed her legs. "Just so you understand, I'm not interested in a man's looks or his money, and I don't care what color he is, or how many times he's been married, or how many kids he has."

"That's comforting," I said, having the feeling she meant it.

Her words formed a welcome diversion from women who wanted sensitive stud muffins with million-dollar bank accounts and men who expected perfect tens. On the other hand, this was over my head.

Rather than waste either of our time, I said, "I'm afraid I specialize in more traditional women. Perhaps some other--"

"No."

"No?"

"Why do you think I'm here?" A tear slipped down her cheek and came to rest on her chin.

I handed her a Kleenex, but she preferred to use a lace hankie from her purse.

Playing out the scenario out of habit, I asked, "What exactly are you looking for?"

She straightened up on the love seat. "Honey, in my case there's only one thing that matters."

"What's that?"

She glanced at me as if I were a slow study. "Acceptance, of course. What else?"

At least she didn't need a reality check. "And in return?"

She assumed a thoughtful pose. "I happen to know how a man thinks and feels better than most women, and I can tell you who won the Super Bowl for the last seven years, and--"

"Wrong."

"What do you mean, 'wrong'?"

"In my six months in business, no man has ever requested an expert on sports' statistics. The words *attractive, slim, nonsmoker.*"

Her expression turned suggestive. "But I'm also quite sexy, don't you agree?"

I stared at her in silence, unwilling to touch that one.

She removed a photo from her purse and handed it to me. My glance roamed from the five-by-eight to her face to the picture again. I was surprised at how much the camera flattered her. A familiar hissing sound distracted me. Turned out her dog was in the middle of marking a section of carpet as his turf.

"Puppy in potty training," she said. She picked up her pet and nuzzled him. "You mustn't get so excited about Mommy having a date."

"Who said anything about a date?"

I grabbed the bottle of Nature's Miracle and roll of paper towels, which I kept in a desk drawer for Sweet Pea's occasional accident, and began to clean up.

"Here, let me help." Alexis dropped to her knees with Puppy underarm.

I pushed her away and finished the job myself.

"So when do we start?"

Although I admired her tenacity and suspected it had enabled her to survive to this point, it made me claustrophobic. "Let me give this some thought."

Her smile shrank like a condom. "How long will that take?"

I stood up again. "Maybe in the future."

She produced a wad of bills. "If it's money you want..." Despite my economically challenged state, I shook my head, feeling too ethical and not desperate enough to accept the cash.

"I'm counting on you." She peeled off a hundred. "I know it won't be easy." She held up another.

"I can't."

She shoved a third hundred in my hand. "I'm lonely."

"And I'm overwhelmed."

She tossed a sheaf of Ben Franklins with steel-point etched backs on the carpet.

I nodded. "I might know somebody."

CHAPTER 3

"A MATCH MUST TAKE LIKE A VACCINATION."

-- *The Matchmaker's Bible*

Alexis Grand required the Personal Introduction of the Year Award. Was I ready for an IRS payment plan? There was something to be said for interest-free money. The trouble was Alexis came with it. Too bad I didn't have a Picasso to unload on eBay.

I stepped over to my mini refrigerator and reached for my chilled magnum of Mumm Cordon Rouge. Never mind I'd been saving it for a special occasion. I needed a drink and it was the strongest thing around.

I popped the cork. The fizz tickled my nose and made me stifle a sneeze. I sank into a chair with my plastic flute and took a sip. The champagne tasted dry, but not too dry. I glanced at Alexis' photo.

The words *long-legged inventor who had reinvented herself recently* came to mind. Isn't that what a spin doctor would say? This could be dangerous. Already I walked a fine line between success and failure, aware that when it came to affairs of the heart, a dissatisfied customer could morph into America's Most Wanted at any time, despite the most thorough vetting process.

My experience with the probation department taught me to listen for red flags, but defer judgment until I could verify the truth, which came in handy in the personal introduction business. I put down my champagne flute, booted up my Mac and typed the words *alternative lifestyles* in the search box of my website. The closest I came was to a man who wanted a woman with enormous breasts. I tried *transgender, cross gender, transvestite, she/male, he/male, she/female, he/female.* A lot of help not. I browsed through my individual client profiles.

Brandon was a fifty-nine-year-old chemist who believed in marriage and had five ex-wives and four daughters to show for it. He described himself as bored by mundane matters and neo- barbarians and sought a smart woman for social and cultural companionship, instead of a push-button lover or instant wife. That sounded like Alexis.

Be still my heart. She just might present the right edge--a match made in who knows where--and my troubles with the IRS would be over. I picked up the phone, punched in Brandon's number and learned he was now in a relationship. I scrolled down to Ryan. He wanted no more children and described himself as open-minded. How open-minded?

I contacted him and mentioned Alexis. "This is simply a bonus, not an introduction."

"Thanks, but no thanks," he said and snickered.

I hesitated. "Even if it's a freebie?"

He shot back, "What is this, some relation of yours?"

"Long-legged, big, prefers dogs to children."

"A dancer?"

"You could say she steps to her own music."

"Modern or classical?"

I knew when to quit. My gaze traveled to *The Matchmaker's Bible,* which I'd snapped up at a garage sale for only a dollar and seventy-five cents and regarded as the Old and New Testaments of personal introductions. I trotted over to my bookshelves and removed the reference from its place between *Cupid's Coach* and *The Ultimate Yenta,* catching a whiff of its rancid stench.

As I cracked open the volume, I heard my janitor wheel in his cleaning equipment. While any number of sanitation engineers could buff, wipe and vacuum, what separated Fong from the rest was his obsession with my plants. I offered him some champagne, but he was more interested in the orchids.

"Mollie's wilting." He frowned. "She needs some special food."

I had no idea which one was Mollie or what he called the others. My neighbor had left three cymbidiums with me before she went out of town.

Fong approached the wastebasket next to my desk and caught sight of Alexis' photo. "Who's that?"

He sported a full head of hair, a smooth olive complexion and pair of laughing eyes. Although Fong seemed to be younger than Alexis, close to a foot shorter and of a different socioeconomic class, he might be a possibility if he weren't the husband of another woman and father of four children. I gave him the scoop on Alexis.

"Sweet." He appeared to be unfazed.

"Too bad you're married."

He nodded, looking forlorn.

I wondered if other Filipino immigrants with Chinese first names would be as liberal in their thinking. Long-legged female physicists with deep voices just might be a selling point for the entire foreign population, in particular, the Third World. Too bad I had only one Swede and two Iranians in my database, but this was L.A., the most diverse city in the nation. I ought to have no trouble finding more immigrants here. Had I underestimated Alexis's marketability? Definitely maybe.

I returned *The Matchmaker's Bible* to the shelf, ran my scanner over her glossy and composed a brief description entitled "Gender Bender with Patents." I wasn't about to pay a computer guru two hundred bucks to develop a new website section or include Alexis with my other female clients, so I created a separate folder.

Meanwhile, I replayed my forty-seven messages. Emily complained that Arthur, her plastic surgeon ex-boyfriend, had demanded his silicon boobs back after she called it quits with him. I should have introduced her to a banker. My telephone burred. I lifted the receiver and exchanged greetings with another client.

"Who's the new beauty?" Zach said. He sounded horny.

It took me a moment to realize he was talking about Alexis. A sci-fi/fantasy-bookstore owner and throwback to the sixties, Zach believed in paying for love these days, to the credit of By Invitation Only. Still single in his fifties, he claimed to want marriage and children. Didn't they all? I filled him in about Alexis.

"It's what she is now that counts. Don't you agree?" Zach said.

"Absolutely." Damn. Did I come on too eager?

"When are you going to introduce us?"

"Actually...she's not a member yet, but I promise to give you first dibs."

"Promise?"

"You bet."

"I'd better get laid soon, or I'm out of here."

"That's not what this is about, Zachary Hoffman."

"Isn't it what ISO means?"

"In search of, m'dear."

"Keep the faith."

Faith, that was it. I contacted Alexis and suggested a second meeting.

That afternoon, Alexis breezed into my office wearing that awful wig and fragrance. Move over, Henry Higgins. My nose and eyes began to water and I reached for the Kleenex box on my desk.

"If we're going to work together, you'll have to accept a makeover, starting with that wig." I blew my nose.

She swept off the wig, revealing a scalp with plugs.

I frowned. "Do yourself a favor. Treat yourself to something more flattering."

"Do you know how much it cost?"

I waved my finger at her. "Men ask what something costs. Women want to know where to find it."

"Do you have a spare?"

I reached in a desk drawer, gathered up my collection of sample fragrances from various Nordstrom's promotions, then dumped them in her hands. "This is the extent of the freebies. Stand up, please."

She bolted to her feet, clutching the perfume vials.

"Turn around."

She did an about-face.

"The dress does nothing for you."

Her soft brown eyes looked wounded. "What's wrong with it?"

"Chartreuse isn't your color."

She pranced over to my guest closet and pulled out a pink Armani, which I had purchased at a final Neiman's sale and kept for emergencies. "This is nice."

I snatched it away. "I'm glad you like it. It's one of my best dresses and it's not on loan."

"What else do you have?"

"You're not dealing with small, medium, large and extra large any longer."

She cocked her head. "You look like an eight."

"Petite."

Alexis dabbed a drop of cologne on her wrists. "I realize I'm no longer a five-speed gear box."

I led her to my love seat.

She said in a wary tone, "Who do you have for me?"

I flopped down at my desk. "A couple of people."

"How do you know?"

"They've told me so. One's a bookstore owner."

"I like to read."

"The other has a way with plants, but he's not available yet. Don't worry. There'll be a lot more once I expand my search."

"What does the thirty-five thousand include?"

"A year of unlimited introductions."

"Not marriage?"

"I never guarantee that."

Silence.

She said with a sigh, "All right, but not a penny more." She unfastened her knockoff Louis Vuitton satchel and pulled out a shitload of money.

I sprang out of my chair. "Alexis, where did you get all that cash?"

"I expect a discount."

I placed my hand over hers. "This ain't Marshall's, you know. A check or credit card will do."

"Half now, the rest at the end of the month."

"That's not how it works here."

"Take it, or leave it."

"Tell the truth. Have you been selling secrets to the Chinese or Hondurans?"

"Don't you trust me?"

I fiddled with the zipper on my jacket. What was there to trust?

Silence.

She arched an eyebrow. "If you must know, I cashed in some of my Apple stock." She began to return the greenbacks to her purse.

Something was better than nothing. The IRS penalties continued to mount. What difference would a couple of weeks make?

"Wait."

She paused.

"As long as you don't tell Marvin--"

She glanced at me innocently. "I wouldn't think of it."

"Okay."

"Okay?"

"Okay.

I wasn't sure how we did it, but we had a deal. I printed out a contract, presented it to her and she signed it. Anxious to get rid of the cash pronto, I shoved the money into a Ralph's market bag and scurried to the bank with it.

Forget pushing one hundred seventy-five bills through an ATM machine. I waited in line for a teller. A woman with big hair called me to a window and greeted me with a supercilious smile. I told her about my intended deposit.

Her smile evaporated. "You need to fill out a special form."

I touched my heart. "I thought you'd be dying to take the cash."

"I'm sorry. It's the government's rule, not ours."

"The government wins, the bank wins and I'm stuck with Alexis Grand."

My Blackberry chimed several bars of Wagner's "Wedding March." I grabbed it, expecting one of my clients.

"No fair," Marvin said. "Why didn't you let me draw up your contract with Alexis?"

"Too late."

"What about my finder's fee?"

"You're on your own, kiddo."

I put away my phone, hoping Alexis was better at fulfilling her financial obligations than keeping secrets.

The next morning, Zach marched into my office with an angry expression that was out of sync with his *Yoga Rules* T-shirt.

He said in an agitated tone, "What'd you do to me? That voice...You didn't tell me about that voice."

"You knew she used to be a man. What'd you expect? She's taking estrogen. It'll change."

He shoved his hands in the pockets of his jeans. "I'm not meeting her, not after that phone call. No way."

"You were the one who suggested it."

"WTF?"

Chill out."

"Chill out? Chill out, my ass." He swiveled around and stomped out with his ponytail swishing.

Go figure liberals. I gazed at the floor having second thoughts about Alexis myself. In the middle of my reverie, the door opened and in walked Fong, grinning.

"What are you so happy about?"

"My wife go to the Philippines."

"For a vacation?"

"No."

"What about you?"

He patted his shiny black pompadour. "Not me."

"I'm sorry."

He began to rubberneck my desk, looking anything but sorry.

"What are you searching for?"

"Where'd it go?"

"You mean the photograph of Alexis?"

A smitten expression crossed his face. I directed him to my photo gallery. He stepped over to her picture and whistled. I had a sudden thought. Under normal circumstances, I wouldn't encourage adultery, but the times were hardly normal.

"Would you like to meet her?"

Concern filled his eyes. "How I pay?"

Little did he know, I considered paying him. "My windows need washing." I shrugged. "And the carpet could use a shampoo."

"What else?"

"As long as you continue to maintain the plants--"

"That all?"

Unwilling to make it too easy, I added, "For now."

"Thank you, thank you, thank you." He grabbed my hand as if he had found the Holy Grail.

I extricated my fingers from his, called Alexis and suggested the three of us meet at a dark Marina del Rey bar overlooking the boats that evening.

Alexis wobbled in on a pair of Christian Louboutin's, looking like an adolescent at her first cotillion. A singer at the piano crooned, "Isn't It Romantic?"

I fixated on her feet. "Aren't those shoes too small for you?"

"You told me to think like a woman. I found them at the resale shop. A bargain's a bargain." She caressed her streaked-blonde wig. "How do you like this one?"

"Much better."

"I rented it," she whispered. "Was it worth it?"

I hesitated. "I can't say."

Her black sheath flattered her figure, and her new fragrance was an odd contrast to the scent of stale booze in the air. I proceeded to introduce her to Fong.

"What a lovely voice you have," Fong said.

She chuckled.

Vulnerability flickered through his eyes. "What so funny?"

She toyed with her pearl choker. "I remember when I used that line on the girls."

This could make me the premiere matchmaker. Justice was blind and so was love. We eased into a booth on the edge of the dance floor. A strawberry blonde on the other side of the room resembled my client Emily. I ducked, wishing I had selected the Santa Monica Mountains during a lunar eclipse for the venue. If she approached us, I could pass off Alexis as pro bono work, a cousin from Kansas or another planet. Yes, another planet.

Suzy, a cocktail waitress with a perky air, scooted over to us. I ordered my usual glass of house merlot, whereas Alexis and Fong preferred Stoli on the rocks. Suzy smiled an ambiguous smile and took off with our order.

"Chloe, is that you?" Emily shouted.

I blew out the candle on our table. Undeterred, she wandered over to us in the compromised light.

I lowered my gaze to her breast implants. "I've been meaning to call. It's none of my business, but they look great. I think you should keep them."

Emily's slender hands cupped her double Ds. "These babies aren't going anywhere. It's Arthur who's history."

Alexis lifted her eyebrows. "I'd kill for those ta-tas."

"Ta-tas?" I kicked her under the table, realizing it was more difficult to change a man's mind-set than his anatomy.

She elbowed me. "What are you kicking me for?"

"It must have been an accident," I said, tempted to gag her.

Emily retreated to her table without an introduction.

Alexis took Fong's arm. "Come on, honey, let's dance."

They melted onto the floor. I wondered who would lead, which seemed like a toss-up, at first. Fong demonstrated more rhythm and didn't seem to mind when Alexis stumbled over his feet. At the end of the music, they returned to the table.

Alexis beamed at him. "Why didn't you tell me you're such a graceful one?"

"That's not all," Fong said in a suggestive tone.

She shot a look at him. "What else?"

"In my country, I'm a veterinarian. Mostly snakes and iguanas."

I sat up with interest. It wasn't often that I found a down-to-earth professional man with as many talents.

As they huddled together in the booth, the prospect of a match filled me with a rush. "When's the next date?"

Fong turned to Alexis. "It's up to the lady."

She stroked his neck. "What did you have in mind?"

"A ride to Malibu?"

"Sure, baby. Your car or mine?"

CHAPTER 4

"A MEAL IS MOST ENJOY-ABLE IN THE COMPANY OF A SOUL MATE."

-- The Matchmaker's Bible

I picked up a Costco barbecued chicken to split with Sweet Pea. We shared the same bed, so why not a six-dollar meal? Except for a pair of cocker spaniel ears, Sweet Pea was all poodle. She fetched her leash from the doorknob, held it in her mouth and wagged her tail. Make no mistake. Her Highness knew what she wanted. I patted her curly black topknot. As I grabbed my keys, she howled with delight. I whisked her outside and into the park, all but deserted except for a couple of ducks, which had wandered over from a nearby lagoon.

During our stroll in the night air, Sweet Pea concentrated on sniffing while I worried about what could go wrong between Alexis and Fong. He could develop buyer's remorse. His estranged wife could find out about Alexis and go ballistic. A 7.6 earthquake could rip apart Pacific Coast Highway, in which case none of it would matter. I led Sweet Pea into the house and served the barbecued chicken. I added kibble to her plate, a green salad and six almonds to mine.

After dinner, I curled up on the couch with the local newspapers and browsed through the *Los Angeles Times* for recruitment opportunities. In the middle of categorizing the deceased into male/female, straight/gay, geographically desirable/undesirable, I felt my eyelids grow heavy and my Sharpie drop from my hand.

A sea of blue diamonds floated through my semi-conscious state, hundreds of them, thousands of them, interspersed with genitalia. Alexis and Fong swam into view.

"Yours, mine, ours?" Alexis asked in a naughty tone.

"I'm pumped," Fong said.

"Me, too. Let's make whoopee."

They sailed to the island of Lesbos and disappeared behind a tower of Vestal Virgins. I awakened with a start. Mary, Mother of Jesus. My watch said four a.m. I sat up and wiped the perspiration from my neck. If I ever took on another pain-in-the-ass client like Alexis again, I intended to charge for nightmares. I lifted myself off the couch and staggered into the bedroom with Sweet Pea. Determined to have better dreams, I concentrated on handing the IRS agent his money. I lifted the comforter over my ears and tried to go back to sleep, but a blue haze haunted me until morning.

Daylight streamed through the shutters. My temples felt as if they had been struck by a hot poker. I stumbled into the master bathroom, downed a couple of Advil, turned on the shower and stood under it until I got a grip. Seventeen, five was a lot of dough, not enough for the IRS but plenty to repaint a townhouse. Tell that to the government.

I dried off, slipped into a turquoise pantsuit and polka- dot T-shirt and grabbed a banana for breakfast. Time to brave the city's multiple potholes. I stopped at a Westchester driving range near LAX on my way to work. Unlike some women who were gym rats, I was a golfer, preferring to commune with nature while working the muscle groups. I deposited my car in a space next to a Mini Cooper and wriggled out of my jacket, which I discarded on the passenger seat so I could swing a club freely. Never mind it was seven thirty in the morning. The eighteen-hole course was already busy. Go figure golfers. I fetched my Lady Cobras from my trunk, changed shoes and tooled over to the pro shop.

The knobby kid behind the counter said, "Got any babes for me?" His eyes were as green as the stripes on his shirt.

I humored him. "When are you going to join?"

"When I get my bird dog fee."

"That might be sooner than you think." I cuffed him on the chin. "Any live ones?"

He riffled through a drawer, removed several slips of paper and coughed them up.

I waved the potential leads in his face. "If any of these pans out as a client, you're in the money, kid."

He frowned. "That's what you always say."

"You got paid once."

He poked his tongue in his cheek.

I winked at him. Hang in there." I shoved the door open door and headed outside.

The air felt crisp. I planted myself at a tee under the overhang and stretched. My neighbors' balls ricocheted past my ears at breakneck speed. I set up a range ball, selected my five iron and took a practice swing. My first shot was perfect, my second wimpy. That was the way with golf. Its intermittent reinforcement kept people coming back for more. I pretended the third shot was Alexis and drove the ball a hundred fifty yards. The fourth and fifth became Marvin and Mother. Enemies were good for the game but bad for life. I hooked a shot, and it landed on the roof of an animal hospital, setting off the ailing dogs. Holy hell. I hightailed it to my car and left the rest of the balls for the next sucker.

By nine o'clock, I was at my Mac comparing the similarities between a traditional Dear John letter and its online equivalent for By Invitation Only's monthly electronic magazine. Regular features included a member's spotlight, announcements and relationship advice, in this case "The Subtle Art of Dumping a Lover by Email."

Alexis phoned to thank me for her personal introduction. "I'm a bit sore, I must admit. We went back to my place last night. I don't know what came over me, but I'm walking bowlegged now."

"Stop with the euphemisms. Did you, or did you not do the deed?"

"Maybe we did and maybe we didn't." She sighed. "We had a couple of drinks and got in the mood and--"

"Don't play coy with me, Alexis."

"I don't care to talk about it."

"Well, you're going to talk about it. Cut the crap. I go to the trouble of setting you up and you do the unthinkable? You know that isn't the way to play it if you want to see the guy again."

Her tone became agitated. "He said he'd call. Do you think he'll call?"

I hesitated. "Would Alex?"

"I don't remember," she wailed.

I hung up the phone in frustration.

My client Madeleine wandered in with a child wearing a Batman mask. "Would you mind watching Jason?"

"Who's Jason?"

She pointed to the little tyke beside her, holding a coloring book and package of crayons.

"I don't think so."

"I have to meet Brian and can't find a babysitter." She exuded an air of desperation. "Jason won't be any trouble. I promise."

"I'm not used to little kids, Madeleine."

"It's only for a couple of hours."

I stared at her. One side of her jaw was less developed than the other, which her long hair partially hid. This was her twelfth introduction. She needed a break and I needed a wedding.

"If it's only for a couple of hours--"

She hugged me and sat Jason in a chair. "Now behave yourself, honey. Be nice while Mommy finds you a daddy." She kissed him and rushed out.

Jason stood up and kicked over an orchid plant. I shoved the dirt back in the pot, worried about what Fong would say. Jason tossed his coloring book aside,

climbed on my desk chair and toyed with the telephone like a raccoon. I grabbed his fingers, beginning
to understand why Madeleine had been unable to find
a babysitter. I told him we were going to have a play
date.

"Where?"

"It's a surprise." I tightened my grip on him and
dragged him downstairs to the parking lot.

I unlocked the passenger door of my eight-year-old
Saab and told him to get in. A Corvette roared down
the alley. Jason broke loose and I ran after him.

"Where do you think you're going?"

"I like to chase cars."

I corralled him into mine.

"Where's your car seat?"

"I don't have one," I said, tempted to lock him in
the trunk.

"Mommy says..."

"Close your eyes and pretend."

I belted him into the back seat. It was a good thing
he was short. I hoped a cop wouldn't be able to see him
and give me a ticket. I took off for the downtown IRS
branch.

There was a diesel spill on the 10 Freeway. I exited
at Crenshaw.

Jason said, "I don't feel good."

I opened his window and pulled over. "Not on the
leather seat."

Too late.

A gardener watered a nearby lawn. I borrowed his hose to clean up Jason and the upholstery and drove to the nearest car wash.

——⊷ ⊷——

The IRS was located in the downtown federal building. I parked in a public lot and led Jason over to the front entrance and into a security line. A clean-shaven guard asked him to remove his Batman mask. Jason refused. When the guard insisted, Jason bit him.

"Holy shit. I hope the little prick doesn't have rabies," the guard said.

"I'm so sorry. He's not mine. Are you all right?"

The guard didn't answer.

I said with trepidation, "I'm here to pay the IRS some money."

A balding man emerged from behind us and called my attention to a drop box on a wall.

"Thanks, but I'd rather deliver it in person."

The expression on his lips was childlike, although the rest of his face had sunk into middle age.

"I'm Hank Buyers," he said in a cheerful tone. "I'm going where you are." He turned to the security guard. "That's okay, they're with me." He escorted us to an elevator.

Jason punched the elevator button and the doors popped open. I stepped inside, keeping my distance from him. Hank pressed six. When the elevator stopped on the right floor, Hank led us into the IRS lobby, down a corridor and to his cubicle. A Pizza Hut menu and Dilbert comic strip hung from a bulletin board. Hank brought in a couple of chairs for us.

"May I get you something?" Hank asked in a solicitous tone.

"No, thanks," I replied, impressed by his consumer-friendly attitude.

I eased into the chair next to his. He requested my social security number. I gave him Mother's and explained the situation.

The corners of his mouth turned up in a smile. "We take pride in our creative financing. You can choose to pay annually, semiannually, quarterly, or monthly. We're one big happy family."

My, my, my. I wondered what he'd eaten for breakfast. I wrote out a check for seventeen thousand, five and handed it to him.

"All I need is a couple of weeks more for the rest of the money. And about the interest and penalties..."

Jason started to draw a mustache on one of the Dilbert faces with a crayon from his pocket. I snatched the crayon away from him.

Hank cleared his throat and looked at me appreciatively. "I hope you don't find this presumptuous of me." He paused. "Each of us has been asked to invite one taxpayer to our annual spring picnic. Would you like to be my guest?"

I was tempted to introduce him to one of my clients. On second thought, this wasn't the time to offend him. At least I knew where he worked and didn't have to worry about an orgy in broad daylight, or him turning into a rapist in front of his colleagues. I imagined a minus fifty percent on his head, and he became more attractive to me.

"I'd love to accompany you."

"Me, too," Jason said.

Hank shook his head. "You're out of luck, young man."

Jason grabbed Hank's finger and sank his teeth into it.

"Ouch," Hank cried.

There was something to be said for having dogs instead of children.

Madeleine met us at my office with a frantic expression. "Where were you? I was about to call the police."

"He bites?"

"Only men...all my husbands when I was married to them."

Jason ran into his mother's arms. "Did you find me a daddy?"

Madeleine beamed at him. "We had such a good time, Brian invited me to dinner with a twofer."

My cell phone rang. I snatched it from my purse and answered.

Alexis said, "You've got to help me, Chloe."

"What's the matter?"

"They think I did it."

"Did what?"

"Killed Fong."

CHAPTER 5

"A MATCH CAN BE DEADLY."

-- The Matchmaker's Bible

I blew off Madeleine and Jason and fled to my car. Had Alexis lost it? How did the cops find out about her? This could put me out of business. I fired up the engine. With any luck, Fong was hit by a truck. Oy vey. What would happen to the seventeen, five she still owed me? It served me right to think the introduction of a five-foot, four-inch Filipino janitor to a lunatic six-foot transgender physicist was the answer to a thirty-five-grand tax penalty.

Why in the hell had I listened to my toxic-waste cousin? Marvin had been getting me into trouble since fifth grade when he stole my Girl Scout money, for which I got blamed and lost a week's worth of *Mickey Mouse Club* television privileges.

Maybe Alexis exaggerated. Maybe Fong wasn't dead. Did I believe it? I wanted to believe he wasn't dead. From Marina del Rey to Brentwood plush, I wove through traffic. I wondered whether Larry, aka Detective Lorenzo Chellini, my ex to the third power, would be part of the homicide investigation. I was in no mood for him to jerk my chain over my match from hell.

Tree trimmers compromised the corals along San Vicente Boulevard with hacksaws. Compromised, I felt compromised, like the corals. I rolled up my windows to muffle the high-pitched grinding noise. I passed the exclusive Brentwood Country Club, where a foursome putted out on a green. Never mind I had been trying to wangle an invitation to play there for months. After that telephone call from Alexis, I had more important concerns than a round of golf. At Bundy, I hung a left, then another at Coyne Lane.

I parked in front of Alexis' fifties-style ranch house, located on a cul-de-sac with mature oaks. As I emerged from my Stockholm special, the pungent odor of freshly cut grass overpowered me like a package of smelling salts. From the absence of patrol cars on the street, I gathered the police had yet to arrive. Breathe in, breathe out. Breathe in, breathe out, or you'll die, too. I strutted over to the entrance banked with pots of impatiens. Alexis met me on the walkway clad in a skimpy T-shirt, pair of shorts and UGG boots.

"I'm so glad you're here," she said, holding Puppy in her arms. The late afternoon light cast a shadow across the dog's blonde coat.

"Where is he?"

She shut her eyes. "I can't bear to go in."

While it was difficult for her, it was difficult for me. Although I had been married to a cop, I had avoided murder scenes like a surgeon's wife with appendectomies. Alexis led me through the living room, decorated in an English country motif, to the master bedroom, where a man lay partially covered under a paisley shawl. One of his legs peeked out from the beaded fringe and lay still, very still. Slowly, the design shifted around his head. It took me a moment to realize it wasn't the shawl but a snake--brown, orange and iridescent--the pattern of which would be attractive on a piece of upholstery. I stopped short in the doorway.

"Alexis, what did you do to him?"

"Nothing, I swear. All I did was invite him over and..."

The dog whimpered. My gaze traveled from Puppy to the snake to Alexis. "Did you try to pry the thing off him?"

She shook her head. "That would take a herpetologist."

I gave her a dubious look. "Isn't there still enough Tarzan left in you?"

She managed a rueful smile. "I've always been more tits than Tarzan."

"May I ask how the snake got here?"

She gestured to an open window. "I took a shower. When I came out..." Her voice caught.

"Could it have escaped from one of your neighbors' houses?"

She shook her head. "Absolutely not."

"What makes you so sure?"

"I'm a transsexual. Remember?"

"What's that got to do with your neighbors?"

She began to sob. "This is terrible. Simply awful."

I shrugged. "It certainly seems like an inefficient way to off somebody."

"Tell that to Fonggie. Poor Fonggie," she wailed.

"How was lunch?"

"We never got around to it."

"Is anything missing?"

"I don't think so." She hiccuped.

The snake chose that moment to extricate itself from the corpse. It slithered off the bed and flowed around the room, keeping its face at eye level and in our direction, with an expression that indicated something was going on inside its head. The question was what?

I tiptoed around it to have a better look at Fong and stared at the ghastly sardonic smile frozen on his lips, which ought to keep me up at least a couple of nights. If this was the world Larry had kept from me, I was grateful now. (If I still felt magnanimous later, I might mention it to him.) A faint sweet aroma emanated from Fong's body. On closer inspection, his neck and shoulders bore scratches and abrasions, which could have originated from a sharp object, instead of a snakebite or squeeze. I waved Alexis over and called her attention to the marks.

She blushed. "I suppose we got a little carried away. We were playing Rock Star and Groupie."

"You were what?"

"He became Bruce Springsteen and belted out the words to 'Born to Run.' I jumped on him and he pretended to protest." She shot a lusty grin at me. "The object was to imagine your greatest fantasy and--"

"I get the point," I said, sorry I asked.

"It's harmless, except for being hell on a manicure." She flashed a couple of broken French tips at me.

I gestured to Fong's neck. "Were those marks there before you decided to take a shower?"

She shrugged. "I didn't notice."

I glanced at Fong's jeans and T-shirt, which lay folded neatly on a chair above a pair of sneakers on the floor. Remembering how some people got off on auto-eroticism, I said, "Was asphyxiation part of your kicks?"

She gave me an indignant look. "Don't be ridiculous."

"Alexis, if Fong specialized in snakes and iguanas in the Philippines--"

"Give me a break."

"Don't be pissed. If I'm asking these questions, I guarantee the police are gonna..."

"I didn't do it." She boohooed into Puppy's fur. "I'm innocent."

The sound of door chimes mixed with Puppy's bark. Alexis left me standing there and returned with two patrol officers--a tan-skinned man and another with unruly eyebrows. They secured the murder scene, pronounced Fong dead and called for backup. I decided against mentioning my ex-husband Larry, unless one of them made the connection, which was unlikely given Larry and I had different surnames.

Shortly thereafter, a pair of homicide detectives arrived. Detective Lyons was a silver-haired man with an easygoing manner, in contrast to Detective Garcia, who exuded an intense air. Garcia began to perspire. I couldn't tell if it was because he was hot, nervous or ill. He mopped his face with his handkerchief and backed away, keeping his eyes focused on the hallway.

"I think I'll wait in the other room," Garcia said.

Lyons intercepted him. "What's wrong, pal?"

"I've got a phobia," Garcia muttered.

I understood now why he was perspiring.

Lyons pulled back his lips in a cynical smile. "Why didn't you say something?"

"When was the last time a snake was part of the protocol?"

Lyons walked circumspectly around the creature. "Looks like a boa. How the hell do you fingerprint it? On second thought, let the crime lab people worry about that shit."

Garcia motioned for Alexis and me to follow him into the hallway. Clinging to the wall, he led us into the living room, where he adopted a business-as-usual manner, apparently more desensitized to death than snakes. Clearly anxious to get rid of the boa constrictor, he contacted Animal Regulation and arranged for a pickup. A forensics photographer showed up with a couple of cameras, followed by a criminalist who wore a small silver hoop in his ear, in contrast to a serious business suit. The first responders brought them up to speed and ushered them to the master bedroom.

Ten minutes later, a size-zero woman appeared, wielding a large burlap sack over her shoulder.

Garcia said in a concerned voice, "They sent you?"

"Nothing to it." She removed a handful of gummy bears from her pocket. "See these?" She marched into the bedroom and returned with the snake in the bag.

CHAPTER 6

"BEWARE OF DRAMA QUEENS FOR CLIENTS."

-- *The Matchmaker's Bible*

Alexis gripped the back of a Queen Anne chair and hung her head. "I can't possibly stay here tonight. I guess I'll have to check into a motel."

"You can stay with me." As soon as I said the words, I had a feeling I was going to regret them.

She rushed over and grabbed me in a hammerlock. "I thought you'd never ask."

"Easy, girl." I peeled her arm off my chest.

The pair of patrol officers entered the living room with Lyons.

He glanced at Alexis through hooded eyes. "Are you left or right-handed, Ms. Grand?"

"I'm ambidextrous," she said with pride.

"I'll bet," he quipped.

"Why?"

"Your boyfriend has a lot of bruises on his neck."

"Who would want to hurt Fonggie?" She turned toward the window sniveling.

"Somebody did. Any witnesses?"

"How would I know?" She hiccuped.

Lyons instructed the patrol officers to chat up the neighbors and closed in on Alexis. "How long did you know Mr. Arroyo?"

She whirled around. "Only a few days." She sighed. "But it seemed a lot longer."

Lyons acknowledged my presence for the first time. "Who are you?"

I extended my hand toward him, but he neglected to take it.

"She's the matchmaker," said Garcia, standing next to an end table.

"Chloe Love." I said in a rapid cadence, "Normally, I conduct a detailed background check on potential clients, but Fong was such a good janitor, and when he wanted to meet her and she wanted to meet him..."

The more I tried to explain, the more ridiculous I sounded to myself.

Lyons crooked his finger at Alexis. "We'd like you to come downtown with us."

She thrust back her head. "The only crime I ever committed was changing gender and this is what happens. I feel...I feel...like an Afghan woman under the Taliban."

I stared at her doe eyes, elevated chin and sixties get up. By the second "I feel," my mind flashed on Jane Fonda in *Barbarella*. "Let's not get carried away, Alexis."

She mocked me with a laugh. "Carried away?"

Lyons said with an edge, "Nobody's accusing anybody."

"What about her?" She narrowed her eyes at me.

"What are you saying?"

Lyons shrugged. "You can ride in the backseat with her."

My gaze snapped to his. "I just got here." I raised my hand in protest. "You have it all wrong. All I did was introduce them."

Alexis cut in. "I demand a female officer."

"You're not really a female."

"How dare you say that?"

"I want a female officer, too," Lyons said. "You take what you get."

"I'm calling Marvin."

"Anyone but him," I protested.

I should have known there were no bargains in this world. Things had gone poorly from the start. Alexis made arrangements to meet Marvin at the station, while I tried to get hold of Larry. Turned out my wusband had gone to Phoenix to pick up a suspect.

Before we left the house, I borrowed a slouchy hat from Alexis, shoved the brim down and put on my dark glasses to disguise my appearance.

We passed a handful of reporters, photographers and neighbors congregated on the sidewalk who came alive like insects under a light.

"Who's the celebrity?" one of the bystanders with a lantern jaw asked.

Alexis paraded in front of him, as if she had Hollywood on the brain. "I'm Alexis, boys."

"No, the other one."

I kept my eyes straight ahead.

"Who killed him?"

"I did," said Alexis. "Wink, wink, nudge, nudge."

I looked at her incredulously. "What's the matter with you?"

"Maybe I'll get some sympathy for a change. I certainly ought to be able to have my pick of lawyers. Who knows? I might even run for the House of Representatives."

I mumbled, "Don't expect my vote."

"Hey, Chloe, what are you doing here?" A man's raspy voice sounded familiar.

I turned my head in time to recognize a scruffy cameraman who tried to join By Invitation Only, until I found out about his domestic abuse conviction and deep-sixed him. He aimed his lens at me.

Alexis elbowed me. "Who's the hottie?"

I whispered, "You have enough problems. Nobody you want to know."

"Chloe what?" the bystander with the lantern jaw said.

"Chloe Love from By Invitation Only," the cameraman said and snickered. "What are you doing here?"

If you can't hide it, you might as well flaunt it. I grinned. "Service is my business."

I shoved Alexis into the LAPD's black and white, praying my sound bite would air after the late-late-late shows, when nobody would be awake.

Garcia leaned inside and locked eyes with Alexis. "Did you kill him?"

"Wink, wink."

"Wink, wink?"

"Don't you get it?"

"Wink, wink, my ass."

I sank into the backseat, aware of the shotguns mounted on one side of the cage and sour smell of upholstery from the unwashed criminal class. Lyons got behind the wheel and started the engine. Our Caprice lurched into the street and bumped along the asphalt.

Alexis batted her eyes at Lyons. "What's it like to work with murderers? Do you have nightmares about corpses?" She leaned against my arm. "I can't imagine..."

I said under my breath, "Please let's keep this on a professional level."

"What is this? A police state?"

I sighed. "Alexis, what are you thinking? Where's your head? Stop acting like a slut."

She muttered, "I know Lyons likes me. Can't you see the way he's staring at me in his rearview mirror?"

"Pipe down back there," he said. "You're giving me a headache."

She bowed her head and fidgeted with her hands. I shot a told-you-so look at her and gazed out the window. Other motorists assessed us with interest. Did anyone recognize me? I felt my stomach somersault. On second thought, after Alexis' performance in front of the press, what was I trying to hide? In a world where celebrity formed the basis of E! Entertainment, a match between a janitor and transsexual, spiced with murder and snakes, ought to be perfect fodder for a TV reality show. What about me? With the free publicity, I ought to be able to land an edgy series, a cross between *The Millionaire Matchmaker, The Bachelor* and *Dr. Phil.*

Lyons chucked the freeway at Temple Street and passed the music center complex. He skirted the paparazzi camped out in front of the station, shot into the underground parking lot and claimed a space reserved for police.

I shimmied out of the car and came around to Alexis' side. She tugged on her shorts, which had hiked up to an indecent level. Lyons and Garcia led us to the entrance, where Marvin waited for us near five sculpted black blobs. Pigs knocked on their sides? Hippos, or bison? Giant molars? Go figure what the artist had in mind. Alexis rushed into Marvin's arms and brought him up to date.

I tapped him on the shoulder. "Remember me?"

He scratched his chin. "Do you need a lawyer, too?"

"Not you, Marvin."

Several hours later, I retrieved my car from Alexis' house, where the media vultures had multiplied.

A disembodied voice said, "I heard someone confessed, something about a snake. Can you confirm it?"

I checked my rearview mirror. A pair of reporters had materialized on my backseat.

"Did he, or she do it?" one said in a nasal tone.

"I believe you're trespassing, boys." I looked at them reproachfully. "Shall I call the police?" I pulled over to the curb and waited for them to get out.

Had Alexis killed Fong? What were the chances of somebody else sneaking through her bedroom window with a sixty-pound boa, in broad daylight, and strangling another person while she lathered up to environmental tapes in the shower? On second thought, the perp might have decided to release the snake outside, and it shimmied up a wall and came through the window all by itself. I left the neighborhood determined to get to the bottom of it.

Jets roared through the darkness as I returned to Playa del Rey. I steered my car into the garage and killed the headlights. The sound of my landline echoed in my ears. I hustled upstairs, dodging Sweet Pea at my feet, and grabbed the living room extension.

Hank Buyers wanted to finalize plans for the IRS picnic. I pondered what I had in my closet that was appropriate for a potato race. So I felt like a hooker. Who didn't now and then? With seventeen, five on the table, at least I was an expensive one. I rushed Hank off the phone, eager to surf the TV channels for news of Alexis and me.

She arrived shortly with Puppy and a suitcase big enough for a week.

"Don't you have anything smaller?" I said, worried about the implications.

Puppy zipped over to Sweet Pea, who backed away growling. He attempted to sniff her behind. Never mind the size disparity between them. Sweet Pea went for Puppy's neck, letting him know who was boss.

"No, Sweet Pea."

She ignored me. I wasn't surprised, since she flunked obedience school twice. I lifted her hind legs. Sweet Pea refused to let go of Puppy. In desperation, I scrambled to my entertainment center and flipped on a Rampal CD, the power of which I discovered the first time I played it and Sweet Pea went into a trance. I held my breath. Rampal hit a very high note. Sure enough, Sweet Pea turned onto her back and began to hum off key with a glazed expression. Flutists appeared to charm special-needs dogs as well as deaf snakes.

"You've been holding out on me," Alexis said.

"I hope you haven't been doing the same on me."

She plopped down on the sectional and removed one of her boots. "This is such a comfortable place."

I snatched her boot away. "Let's not get too comfortable." I led her into the guest room and hesitated in the doorway. She pulled off her wig and fluffed it.

"Did you?"

"Did I what?"

"Did you murder him?"

"Of course I didn't fucking murder him."

She stood there swearing like a bald sailor with tits but exuding an authentic air.

CHAPTER 7
"KNOW YOUR CUSTOMER."
-- The Matchmaker's Bible

Alexis and I trolled through the TV stations. Still no news about us. My stomach felt empty. I checked my watch. It was close to eight o'clock at night. I handed the remote control to Alexis and stepped into the kitchen to explore the dinner fixings. A can of tuna, box of cherry tomatoes, dozen eggs and package of almonds were enough to feed, if not stuff, us. I began to set the table with a couple of place mats.

The smell of nail polish wafted into the dining room from the sunken living room. I leaned over the rail to have a look. To my chagrin, Alexis sprawled on my area rug, touching up her manicure.

I gasped. "Can't you do that somewhere else?"

She returned the wand to the bottle of red lacquer and surveyed her fingernails. "I'm sorry. Whenever I'm nervous, I have to polish my nails."

Before she had time to tackle her toes, I charged downstairs to check for drips.

Alexis kept her eyes on the TV. "They keep talking about a heightened security alert."

"Lucky us."

"Who knows if it's real or made up? Fonggie's dead and that's real." Alexis reached for the nail polish.

"Enough coats," I said emphatically.

Puppy lifted a hind leg. I grabbed him and rushed him to the sink, listening for a trickle. What had begun as a short commitment was beginning to feel like a thirty-year fixed loan.

"Did he go?"

"No." I deposited Puppy in Alexis' lap. "You'd better take him out."

While they were gone, I made a couple of tuna fish sandwiches and whipped up a tomato and onion frittata for us and scrambled some eggs for the dogs.

The front door swung open and Alexis stumbled in with Puppy. "Something smells good."

"I hope you like eggs."

"Just the yellows."

"I guess you'll have to cope." I removed the frittata from the stove and brought it to the table. "What do you want to drink?"

"A beer."

"With eggs?" I gave her a skeptical look.

"Make it scotch on the rocks."

During dinner, she knocked back two stiff ones during dinner, most of the frittata, both tuna sandwiches and a quart of Starbucks mocha almond fudge, then belched up a nasty blend of smells.

"Pardon me." She tapped her lips.

"Coffee?"

"Make it another Cutty Sark."

I appealed to her vanity. "You look a little puffy."

"Where?"

"Around the eyes."

"You think so?"

"I know so. You've had enough." I snatched her glass away. "What else can you tell me about Fong?"

She examined herself in the dining room mirror. "He was well hung."

"Beside that."

"Uncircumcised."

"Alexis, a woman is supposed to care more about a man's sensitivity than his anatomy. Think. Did your boyfriend appear to be concerned about anyone or anything?"

"I was only at his house once," she said offhandedly.

"What house? He rented a house?"

"I think he owned it."

I started to clear the table, but her words nagged at me. Anxious to perform an overdue background check on Fong, I produced a bottle of Palmolive and handed it to her.

"Feel free to wash a few plates."

"Do you have any gloves?"

"Nothing in your size."

I headed upstairs to my laptop and went online. Yahoo listed Fong's address in the historic West Adams district, once an upscale neighborhood, now where USC Trojan fans paid twenty dollars to park on lawns before football games. I checked the multiple-listings book to verify the name of the owner. Sure enough, Fong shared title with a woman named Juanita Arroyo, whom I assumed was his wife. Granted the home wasn't in the best part of town, but nothing in L.A. was less than three hundred K. Even if they bought low, they must've come up with a down payment and qualified for a loan. How had my janitor and his wife scraped up the money?

Thursday's *Los Angeles Times* printed nothing about Alexis and me. Still, it was less than twenty-four hours since her command performance in front of the media and the city was on heightened security alert. After polishing off the rest of the frittata, three defrosted bagels and several cups of decaf, Alexis announced she was ready to go; I didn't ask where. I followed her around the house to make sure she left nothing behind, including Puppy.

I stripped her bed, gathered up her sheets and towels and left them for the maid to wash. Never mind a cash-flow problem. Whenever I did the laundry, it developed holes. Better to play golf, except when it came to murder. If Alexis didn't kill Fong, who did? I cancelled my standing tee time that morning to do some investigating in my late janitor's neighborhood.

After a shower, I turned on CNN for company while I got dressed. In the middle of hooking my bra, I heard that a Los Angeles transsexual had confessed to killing her lover. Aha. Our one-and-a-half minutes of fame had arrived. I stepped over to my Sony.

Alexis danced down the avenue with me at her side. In the slouchy hat and dark glasses, I looked like Humphrey Bogart in *Casablanca*. Too bad it wasn't Ingrid Bergman. I switched stations. Again it was Alexis and me.

My landline and cell phone rang in unison. I snatched them up. Arthur wanted no part of murderers and suspended his By Invitation Only membership, effective immediately. Emily insisted upon a full refund. This didn't look good for the rent. Attempting to take my mind off the future, I let the rest of my calls go to voice mail and threw on a pair of sweats and flip-flops.

The streets in the West Adams district radiated vibrancy from immigrants preoccupied with the American dream instead of IRS loopholes, expensive personal introduction services and sex- change operations. Fong's two-story Victorian backed up to the Vermont on-ramp of the Santa Monica Freeway. I snapped a couple of pictures with my cell phone camera. Unlike other properties on the block with sagging porches, graffiti and parched lawns, Fong's house was freshly painted and sported a front door with a stained-glass inset. During USC football games, he could've gotten away with charging an extra fin for parking on his lawn. Why hadn't Alexis made a point of mentioning more about his spread? I got out and gazed at the colored-glass shards idly. He had been well hung and well heeled, unless *Restore America* had intervened. How else could he afford such a home? I started up the walkway.

"Nobody's there," a man with a macaw on his shoulder said from the portico of the next-door apartment building.

My gaze lingered on his macaw. Out of the corner of my eye, I saw an array of black and whites invade the street. I froze. They pulled up in front of Fong's home. A bunch of cops rushed out and surrounded me with guns.

I raised my hands in the air, trembling. "Don't shoot."

"Hey, don't I know you?" one of the boys in blue said, staring at my puss.

In their uniforms, they all looked alike to me.

He took a couple of steps toward me.

A woman across the street shouted, "Wrong house."

He and the others lost interest in me and dashed over to the woman across the street. I lowered my arms to my sides. Three men and another woman, half-dressed, spilled out of an apartment building's side window. I wasn't about to stick around to chat up the cop who thought he recognized me. Convinced no one would allow a house like Fong's to remain empty for long, I left my business card on his door, curious about what it would yield.

I picked up my email messages from the road. Nine more clients and three potential ones had bailed on me. Without a new infusion of capital, I might be eating Science Diet with Sweet Pea before the end of the week. My stomach whirled like a washing machine. I counted on recruiting some fresh meat at a singles fair that evening. To entice potential customers, I planned to give away a trip to Maui, compliments of my frequent flyer miles and Marriott rewards points. I just hoped there'd be enough open-minded people in attendance to justify the four hundred dollars I'd forked over for a booth.

Never mind a deluge of calls from clients, acquaintances, friends and reporters on my phones. I rushed home and dragged out a Hawaiian DVD from my entertainment center, then freshened up for the evening. I attached a Swarovski heart-shaped crystal broach to the lapel of my final-sale Armani, stepped into a pair of fuck-me pumps and grabbed my purse. Although I contemplated stopping by Fong's house to see if my business card had been removed from the door, I decided to give it more time.

I self-parked at the Beverly Hilton Hotel, hiked my purse over one shoulder and marched through the lobby to the ladies' room, where I ran into one of my competitors speaking on her mobile next to a sink. Polly appeared to be oblivious to anyone overhearing her. Her breasts ballooned above a gold lame' strapless number, which emphasized the crepe-paper texture of her cleavage.

She angled her head toward me, put away her cell phone and hurled a disapproving look at me. "I resent you giving matchmakers a bad name, Chloe Love. How could you take on a murderer?"

"I did no such thing."

Polly wagged a bejeweled finger at me. "Shame on you. "Are you trying to ruin it for all of us?"

A hotel clerk drying her hands with an automatic blower stole a glance at us.

I continued to go toe-to-toe with Polly, although I wanted to cry. When she answered another call in her diva voice, I ducked out of there and headed for the grand ballroom. I set up shop between a financial planner specializing in single women and a travel agency featuring trips without solo supplements.

The double doors parted for the first arrivals. I started my promotional DVD and forced a smile. Aloha. I spotted my client Zach across the room. At least I hoped he was still my client, given the way things had been going lately. Attired in a pair of slacks, sport shirt and jacket, he looked more like an attractive businessman than VW-bus refugee, which was his usual persona. He ambled over to me with a determined gait. Was I about to lose another customer? Not without a fight.

I complimented Zach on his appearance.

He said in a droll tone, "Yes, I do clean up well. Hey, what's this I hear about Alexis Grand?"

"I don't think she's guilty."

"No?"

I shook my head. "No matter what you've heard."

He smiled a winsome smile. "Don't worry. You're not getting rid of me so fast."

Anxious to steer the conversation away from murder, I shoved a pen in his hand and urged him to fill out the entry blank for the Hawaiian vacation. He continued to hold the pen. The DVD stopped working, and a plane stuck in midair on its descent into the Honolulu airport. I flicked off the machine. When I turned around, Zach was gone. I wasn't sorry. At least, he was still aboard. A steady stream of lookyloos replaced him.

A woman with a double chin said, "You take killers?"

"It's only a rumor."

"Do you know anybody who likes large women?"

I gave her the once-over, felt a hand on my shoulder and turned quickly in its direction, resulting in a whiff of my favorite ex- husband's citrus-scented cologne.

"Any idea where I can find a good introduction service?" Larry flashed a devilish smile at me.

The ruddiness of his complexion intensified the blue of his eyes. His chestnut hair, never abundant, was thinner, and the creases around his mouth had deepened to jowls, which filled me with satisfaction.

"Care to have dinner?" he asked in his familiar soothing baritone.

"Been there, done that, thanks." I fidgeted with an entry blank.

"Wouldn't mind doing it again," he said with a wink.

"Yeah?" From the way he tugged on his tie, I knew he had heard about Fong Arroyo. "Have you talked to Lyons and Garcia?"

Silence.

"I'm worried you've transformed into a ringmaster in a circus."

"You ought to know I'm no clown act."

"Maybe not," he said with a shrug. "But that sideshow act of yours was taken into custody this morning."

"Alexis Grand?"

He nodded.

"For more questioning?"

"I think they booked her."

I felt a tingle of apprehension. "Have they had an autopsy yet?"

"What difference does it make?" He shook his head. "People like that should never have been born."

"You're generous in spirit today, a true Christian. Did you ever consider applying to the United Nations?"

"I had to be a diplomat to be married to you."

I didn't go to dinner with Larry. I closed up shop early and drove by Fong's house. It was still daylight, but the porch light was on. Did it operate on an automatic timer? I could see from the street that my card had been removed from the door.

CHAPTER 8

"BE CAREFUL OF FELONS FOR CLIENTS."

-- *The Matchmaker's Bible*

B efore I headed over to the holding tank the next day, I checked its visiting hours and jotted down the address. I heard on my car radio something about a plot to blow up some local buildings. I didn't pay much attention, preoccupied with what Alexis had to say for herself.

I drove my little Inge to the San Fernando Valley, marveling at how quickly I had gone from setting up people at Café Marina to showing up at a Van Nuys lockup facility. The personal introduction biz certainly defied description. I tuned in an FM station and chilled out on some easy-listening jazz. Construction reduced Coldwater Canyon to one lane. Elvis Costello crooned, "It's delightful. It's delicious. It's de-lovely." I didn't feel delightful, delicious, de-lovely. I felt responsible for a costly mismatch.

Soon pricey estates gave way to tract homes and marble yards. A radio newscaster announced the cancellation of the downtown St. Patrick's Day parade due to a bomb plot. Bomb plots, schmomb plots. My thoughts shifted to Alexis. It was her own fault she had been arrested. Was she guilty?

At Victory Boulevard, the panorama changed to Hispanic mom-and-pop stores, low-income housing and schools with the current version of the Valley girl. Less than a mile away, I came upon a large sandstone rectangle with bars on the windows. Go figure why the city decided to put a holding tank in the middle of a residential community. I slowed down. A sign on the building said VAN NUYS CORRECTIONAL FACILITY.

I lifted my foot off the accelerator and swung into a lot on the corner of Sylvan and Van Nuys. A woman backed out of a spot, which I nabbed before somebody else grabbed it. I killed the motor and phoned my office. Whoever had removed my card from Fong's door had yet to call. I set my car alarm and trekked past an old Caddie, kid on a bicycle and woman in a sari.

A disembodied female voice in the building cried, "I love you."

"I hate you," said another.

"Bitch," said the first one.

I stood there a moment, absorbing the despair around me, then strode into the lobby. A young fellow with a pronounced Adam's apple gave me the once-over. Get a life. Another with a scar above his lip whistled under his breath. Nobody was shy here. I complied with a sign on the wall and left my cell phone with a deputy at the information desk. Her irregular features qualified as almost pretty, rather than beautiful. The air felt warm and still. I removed my Armani jacket--no bargain now like its matching dress--and queued up with lovers, husbands, wives, boyfriends, girlfriends, parents, kids, pimps and lawyers waiting to pass through the security system. I submitted to a body search and followed another female deputy, whose expressionless face was like a troll's, into a visitor's room. I settled into a chair next to a table, stepped out of my nude pumps and massaged my tootsies while I waited for Alexis to surface on the other side of the Plexiglas.

She shuffled in looking like a guy, despite the forty K she'd blown on reassignment.

"Where have you been?" Alexis stood there in orange prison jumpsuit and shackles, without benefit of wig and makeup.

"Since when am I your keeper?"

Her eyes challenged mine. "Honey, I've had more propositions in the last hour...The problem is they're the wrong gender."

What was the right one?

She said with a desperate note, "I called Marvin and told him to get me out of here."

"You called him?"

She sat down gingerly. "Gloria Allred's supposed to be over-rated and..."

"Compared to Marvin?"

She glanced at the deputy behind her and said with a deep sigh, "Guard, guard, I want my dog."

The guard, a big-boned woman, said in a patronizing tone, "Think of it like a restaurant. No dogs allowed."

I stared at my client, worried she was having a meltdown. "Where is Puppy?"

"With Marvin."

"I hope he doesn't kill him," I said, recalling how Marvin had hanged his hamster when he was six.

Alexis shook her head. "Those bastards have been so rough on me here. They think I know something about blowing up some buildings. Have you ever heard of anything so ridiculous?"

I leaned forward. "Do you?"

"What do you take me for?"

⊨⊨ ⊨⊨

Alexis had enough problems without being a terrorist--murderer maybe, terrorist no. Still, stranger things have happened. What about Fong? When he saw Alexis' picture on my desk and asked to meet her, how much did he know about her being a scientist? Never mind his clean-shaven face and bare head. Could he have been Osama bin Waterer? It would explain the FBI's line of questioning of Alexis, and it would explain Fong's obsession with her beyond a pair of long legs and deep voice. I crept through traffic, like the other martyred drivers in L.A., wondering how I'd missed the clues. Fong had been in the habit of humming Cat Stevens' "Moon Shadow" around the plants. Holy Krakatoa. Was he an eccoterrorist?

I pulled up to Fong's home and turned off the motor. Azaleas, roses and daffodils were in bloom out front, stirring my misgivings about him. A couple of teenage boys slipped out of the next-door apartment building, where the man with the macaw had been during my last visit. Twilight wasn't the best time to be wandering around Eighty-eighth Street and Vermont, yet I had to assuage my curiosity. Laughing, shouting, pushing, the boys gave me a dismissive glance, careened up the block and into another yard. I hoisted myself out of the car, set the alarm and moseyed up the path to the front steps, catching a whiff of the fragrant landscape.

I peered through the screen door at a handful of women in headscarves who were chatting in what could be Tagalog. They occupied a sofa, surrounded by plants. It was as if I were watching a foreign movie dubbed in the wrong language.

"Does anyone speak English?" I leaned my forehead on the screen door.

A diminutive woman with Asian features stood up, cackling. "We speak American."

The other ladies snickered. Regretting my question, I introduced myself and offered my heartfelt condolences.

The diminutive woman met me at the door.

"Mrs. Arroyo?" I said

"What's it to you?"

I felt my teeth clench, but smiled at her. "When did you get back from the Philippines?"

"Are you one of his, too?"

So that was it. "Oh, no. No, no, no. You've got the wrong idea."

She unlatched the screen door and dragged me inside. "Prove it."

"Your husband wasn't my type. Besides, I've been celibate for years."

She grabbed a handful of sympathy cards from a sideboard and thrust them on the floor. "What's with all these Anglo chicks?"

I lifted my gaze from the array. A girl, no more than seven or eight assessed me with Fong's dancing eyes. She even combed her hair in a pompadour like his. Fong's widow left the room and returned with a cookie on a napkin, which she shoved in my hand. It smelled like cinnamon. I broke off a small piece and hesitated.

Fong's widow nudged my hand. "What are you afraid of? Do you think I'm going to poison you?"

"Yes," I blurted out, locking eyes with hers.

The girl ran into the kitchen and emerged with a fistful of the golden-brown squares. "See, it's safe."

She downed them two at a time, appearing to be more concerned with pigging out than convincing me on their appeal.

Silence.

"If I wanted to kill you, I wouldn't bother with arsenic," Fong's widow said in an animated voice. "We have Uzis in this country."

"Hear, hear, Juanita," the other women chanted, like the three witches in *Macbeth*.

Juanita guided my arm toward my lips. "Eat."

If I died, I hoped it would be over quickly. I took a bite. It tasted like matzo. Pui, feh. I wiped my mouth with the napkin. Juanita yanked it away from me, sending the rest of the cookie to the floor. She rushed into another room with the napkin. Had I just met the green widow or black one? I kneeled down to wipe up the crumbs and came upon a copy of the Qu'ran leaning against a rolled-up rug near the base of a sideboard.

Juanita returned to the room with a satisfied smile. "You're lucky it's the wrong color, lady."

I raised myself to my full height and shot a menacing look at her.

She said petulantly, "My husband was always coming home with different shades of lipstick. After the tenth or fifteenth time, I could have killed him myself." The corners of her mouth turned down in a pensive expression. "Why couldn't it have been me who murdered the SOB?"

My head was spinning. I tried to rein in my thoughts. He might not have been a terrorist, but he was certainly a philanderer with an untraditional wife.

CHAPTER 9

"DO AS I SAY, NOT AS I DO."

-- The Matchmaker's Bible

A broadcast originated from a mosque on Vermont Avenue, inviting people to a prayer service. Actually, it sounded more like karaoke to me. The mosque was only a few blocks from Juanita's house. Did she belong here? I parked in the lot of the blue-and-white tile building with an imposing gilt dome. The smell of pizza from a Domino's next door almost derailed me. I continued to the steps, where a man dressed in a flowing robe and skullcap exuded the air of an imam in his interactions with some men in a corner. I waited for him to finish and tried to strike up a conversation with him, but he wasn't the friendly type.

━◦━ ◦━

Before I turned in for the night, I made some notes on my laptop. Fong owned fancy house in the hood with a prayer rug and Qu'ran in sight. Probably Muslim like Juanita, although danced, drank and cheated on wife. Claimed to be a veterinarian in the Philippines. No animals in sight, only a lot of living plants and flowers and three ladies in headscarves. Where were his other children? Somebody wanted him dead. Who were his enemies? Beginning to sound like a bit of a scumbag. More information needed. Start with another visit to his widow.

━◦━ ◦━

I telephoned Juanita Arroyo and arranged to meet her after lunch the next day, which gave me time in the morning to upgrade my client Roger's basic package to a more lucrative personal recruitment one, since he'd been through all my accomplished thirty-to-thirty-five-year-old drop-dead-gorgeous brunettes and was too busy to seek out his own candidates.

Patricia, a serial monogamist, and Robert, a serial dater, popped into the office to announce their engagement. I congratulated them, delighted with the news of By Invitation Only's first wedding. Since I'd consumed most of the Mumm Cordon Rouge myself, I resorted to a new bottle of Cook's champagne in my refrigerator to celebrate the occasion. It tasted young, but not brash, requiring no apologies. I heard footsteps in the lobby and excused myself.

A hunk stood in the lobby. Be still my heart. With those biceps, he was quite the stud muffin. I wondered what he was doing here, not that I was complaining.

"Good morning," I said with an enthusiastic lilt.

He twitched a smile. "Ms. Love?"

"Yes."

He shoved a badge in my face. It appeared to be three feet by five. Holy crap. This was a match of a different kind.

I spilled champagne on my hands. "Do you expect to come in here with that thing and frighten me?" I shook the drops off my fingers.

Mr. America removed a camera from his belt case and produced a digital shot of me in front of a mosque, while I engaged in heated conversation with the imam. I gazed at the hunk, at the photo and at him again. Suddenly, his face became ugly.

"This is you, isn't it?" His gray eyes projected a gotcha expression.

"It's not even my good side." I crossed my arms in front of me and rocked back on my heels. "I see you've been following me. May I ask what this is about?"

Patricia and Robert joined us with their bubbly. I shooed them out, promising to resume our celebration at another time. The hunk provided me with a manila envelope entitled HOMELAND SECURITY OFFICIAL BUSINESS. I unsealed it and saw the words *Search Warrant, SearchWarrant, Searchhh Warrant.*

I lifted my eyes to his. "What do you think you're going to find?"

He glanced over my head. "May I see your computer, ma'am?"

"I have nothing to hide." I led him into my inner office.

He reached inside his jacket pocket and produced a miniature screwdriver from a small plastic case.

"Wait just a minute." I hugged my Mac. "What are you doing? First the police, now you. All my records--I hope you're not planning to--Take my backup drive."

"That, too."

I let go of the machine. "Is this some type of setup?"

He asked if I had been conversing with a terrorist group called Abu something.

"Abu...Abu who?"

"We've traced their messages to your computer."

"You've hacked into my computer?"

He leaned over the keyboard and pulled up something in Arabic.

"What's that?"

He continued in a no-nonsense tone. "Are you into metric scones?"

"Huh?"

With a few more strokes, he brought up a series of formulas. "Are these yours?"

"In your dreams."

"Who else has access to your computer?"

"This is a one-person office."

He fiddled with more keys and brought up a map of the city with rings drawn around the Los Angeles Convention Center, Staples Arena and L.A. Live Entertainment Complex. The title of the map: "Down with Capitalist Rogues."

"How'd that get there?" I shoved my fist in my mouth.

"Have you been following the news?"

"Omigod." I hesitated. "You mean that terrorist plot to blow up part of downtown L.A.? You don't think I...I know anything about...do you?"

His expression was enough of an answer. My stomach felt queasy. Again the inmates were running the asylum. The only other person with a key to my office was Fong and he was dead. The hunk handed me his business card and ordered me to get in touch with him, in case I decided to leave town.

I dumped the plastic champagne flutes in the trash and opened the windows to let in some fresh air. The hunk neglected to ask if I had another computer. It was none of his business anyway. I trudged downstairs, dragged my laptop out of the trunk of my car and upstairs to my desk, where I went online and looked up terrorist groups.

According to Wikipedia, Abu was a popular name. There was the Abu Nidal, whose bases of operation were in Iraq, Libya and Syria, not here. That didn't sound right. Abu Hafs functioned in Spain only. Pass. I scrolled down to Abu Sayyar, which had originated in the Philippines and had cells around the world, including the United States. Fong was from the Philippines. I focused on its mission statement, which was to purify Islam through kidnappings, bombings, beheadings and assassinations. Was that what the hunk had been talking about? Yikes. It felt like a match. I couldn't find anything about Fong Arroyo. Then again, how many jihadists went by Joe, Billy Bob, Lucille, or Fong?

I fortified myself with a Starbucks tall decaf before subjecting myself to Fong's preternatural widow that afternoon. The Santa Monica Freeway was unusually open. The notion of my late janitor's involvement in Abu Sayyar certainly put a different spin on things, including how Alexis fitted into the puzzle. I reached for my Beach Boys CD and tripped out on "Surfing USA". Surfing, I was surfing the murky waters of murder. I zipped over to Vermont Avenue and made a couple of quick rights to Fong and Juanita's fancy anomaly in the hood. The street was being cleaned, so I parked around the corner. I was close to fifteen minutes early for my appointment with Juanita but sprang out of my car, unwilling to hang with the homeboys and girls. Bus fumes assaulted my nostrils, chasing away my sand-and-sea state of mind. I fed the meter, rounded the corner and knocked on Juanita's door.

She surfaced in the doorway, wearing an Epcot Center T-shirt and said, "I'm about to make cookies for the mosque bake sale. Wanna lick the bowl?" She gave me a cunning smile.

My throat constricted at the memory of my last tasting experience with her. Still, I played along and hauled myself into the large white kitchen with stainless steel appliances. The room smelled like ammonia, which explained its spotlessness. She removed a nest of mixing bowls from a central island cabinet. A burlap sack rested against the island.

"That's quite a big bag of flour you have."

"We're trying to raise enough money to buy explosives."

What was the deal with these two? As crazy as she was, she couldn't be that blatant about her intentions, or could she?

"I think your husband was using my computer to conduct terrorist activities," I said in a carefully modulated voice.

She looked at me with a scary smile. "First, I must purify my instruments. It takes all my concentration."

I glanced at the sack on the floor. The label on the front said CAUTION: HIGHLY FLAMMABLE. ORGANIC FERTILIZER. I flinched. For all I knew, Fong had been working for his wife.

I got the hell out of there and climbed into my car. Juanita probably belonged to Abu Sayyar, like her late husband. I stepped on the accelerator and joined traffic along Vermont Boulevard. How much did the Feds know about her antics? I felt compelled to tip them off. On second thought, I was in enough hot water with Homeland Security. Better to contact them anonymously. I considered texting the hunk, but he might be able to trace the message to my BlackBerry.

There must be a public phone left in this city. Since the advent of mobile technology, I'd become as desensitized to them as a vegan to Fatburgers. I cruised along Adams, cut across Crenshaw and caromed through Leimert Park, center of the local African-American arts scene. I passed a coin-operated laundry, Baptist church, Walmart, several clubs. Still, no sign of a phone booth.

I was contemplating shelling out fifteen bucks for a pre-paid phone when I spotted two relics from the past in front of a strip mall. Too bad I was in the wrong lane to stop. I went around the block, parked beside a chili joint and scooped up my meter money from the car's ashtray.

An unsavory character attempted to help a woman start up an old clunker next to me. The clunker began to idle. I slipped past them to the street. Graffiti artists had given both booths equal time with spray cans. One instrument required thirty-five cents to make a local call, the other fifty. A lot of sense not. I selected the bargain, which smelled like puke. Feh. I deposited my money. Dial tone. Now all I needed was something to muffle my voice. I checked my purse. Sweet Pea had gotten into my package of Kleenex, so I took off one of my socks. I scoped the area for spectators. No cameras, please. I wrapped the sock around the mouthpiece, ferreted out the hunk's business card and dialed his number. A receptionist answered in a high-pitched voice. I gave a fictitious name and asked to speak to the hunk. A couple of moments passed. I heard a click on the line and then his voice.

"About Juanita Arroyo--"

"Ms. Love?"

"Who?"

"The matchmaker Chloe Love."

I began to schvitz. "What gives you that impression?"

"I'm looking at your photo in front of the Isa Mosque."

"Isa what? You have the wrong person."

He hesitated. "You certainly sound like..."

I plunked down the receiver. Shit. That hadn't gone well. I felt outed, backed in a corner with no place to turn, in need of investigating a whole new set of murder suspects on my own. I slipped the sock on my foot again and skulked to my car. The clunker next to it was gone. I scooted into my Saab, backed out of the lot and headed toward Playa del Rey.

My Bluetooth startled me. Holy Ishram. Was the hunk calling back? Turned out Zach wanted to meet me for a drink. Better him than the hunk. I suggested a tapas bar on Abbot Kinney, a trendy street named after the developer of Venice, California and its canals.

＝‡ ‡＝

In the subdued light, I shouldered my way through a happy-hour crowd to Zach, who waited for me at one of the rough-hewn wooden tables.

He pulled out a chair for me, which scraped the floor and I winced. "You look beat."

I gave him a fleeting smile.

He sat down next to me and steepled his hands on the table. "Tell me all about it," he said in a nurturing tone.

I reached for a Spanish olive from a complimentary dish on the table. "I'd rather not discuss it, if you don't mind."

"That bad?"

I popped the olive into my mouth and savored its oily taste. A guitarist played flamenco music in a corner. Although I was desperate to talk to somebody, I still had enough brain cells left to keep from unloading on a client.

He took my hand and squeezed it. "You can trust me."

I snatched my fingers away, grabbed my cell phone and offered up the number of my flight-attendant client who was preoccupied with elves, fairies and angels, which ought to mesh with a fantasy bookstore owner's stock and trade. "Call this lady."

He smiled a provocative smile. "We could make a lovely life together."

"You and Ruth?"

"You and me."

At fifty, I'd come to feel invisible to men, and it took me a moment to recover from the occupational hazard of being hit on by a client.

He said, "Don't look so surprised."

I gazed at the yellow ring around each of his pupils and patted his arm. "If you weren't my client..."

"C'mon. Don't you ever make an exception?"

I shook my head. "I'm the matchmaker, not the match."

⚒ ⚒

Hank Buyers showed up for the IRS picnic on Sunday morning, wearing a muscle shirt, cutoffs and Dodgers cap. I hardly recognized him without his coat and tie. I followed him to his boxy black-and-chrome dinosaur across the street.

"How do you like it?" he said with a proud grin.

I shrugged. "As long as there isn't a bomb under the hood..."

His brow creased in a wavy pattern. "What makes you say such a thing? Do you know who drove it?"

I shook my head.

"Henry Ford II."

"What is it?"

"An Edsel."

As I slid inside, my legs stuck to the seat. "Is this vinyl?"

"The original. Cost me thirty thousand to restore. Isn't it cherry?"

I neglected to tell him it was the ugliest car I had ever seen. Overcome by the hooker feeling again, I shoved my arm out the window. He revved the engine and pulled away from the curb.

"There's something I'd like to discuss with you. A little business matter."

He clapped my shoulder. "Today's a day for fun."

I said through clenched teeth, "Yes, I know, but I was wondering if you could do me a little favor." I removed my sunglasses and blinked at him.

He stopped for a light. "We have plenty of time to talk later."

I nodded with resignation. He maneuvered on to the Santa Monica Freeway and floored it. We must have been doing twenty-five miles per hour.

"You're quite the speed demon," I said, jerking forward in my seat.

"I used to race motorcycles."

I grinned at him, hoping his enjoyment of living on the edge would translate to sympathy for taxpayers in need of special consideration.

He exited the freeway at Overland and continued along Pico to Beverly Hills. Near Roxbury Park, Hank slowed down to fifteen miles per hour. He entered the parking lot and came to a stop between a pair of Priuses. He got out and wiped the chrome trim on his Edsel with a cloth, then came around to the passenger side and helped me out. He removed an ice chest and blanket from the backseat.

"I'm in charge of sandwiches."

"Chicken liver?"

"What gave you that idea?"

"You've had some effect on mine lately."

He chuckled. "Trust me. I'm harmless."

That remained to be seen. He reached inside the trunk for something, which turned out to be a toaster oven.

"I fixed it for a friend. My specialty is Electroluxes. Do you have any appliances not working?"

"Not at the moment. Maybe in the future." I gave him a polite smile.

We trudged through the grass toward a section of picnic tables with balloons and an IRS banner. Hank contributed his sandwiches to the potluck and returned the toaster oven to a lady with a bald spot on the back of her head. The smell of charcoal wafted from a nearby barbecue pit, where another man, whose girth resembled a sumo wrestler's, grilled hot dogs, hamburgers and chicken. I helped myself to Cobb salad and fresh melon, while Hank opted for liverwurst on rye and potato chips.

We settled next to an oak tree with our plates. I heard something move behind us, turned my head in its direction and came face to face with a snake. I shrieked.

Hank laughed. "Are you one of those girlie girls?"

The snake was brown and small. I bolted to my feet and gravitated to another tree, where I picked at my salad. Hank followed me there.

He gave me a sideways glance. "So what was it that you wanted to talk about?"

I paused. "Getting back to that little favor, I've had a lot of people after me lately and business hasn't been so good. I wonder if you could shuffle around a few papers...just for a couple of months...place my file on the bottom of the stack."

He wiped his lips with a napkin. "Oh, I'm sorry. Didn't I tell you? They've given your case to my friend Arnold. Come, let me introduce you." He dragged me over to the sumo wrestler at the barbecue. I preferred to sacrifice my first-born, rather than ask for any help from him, afraid of being sat on.

There was a loud explosion in the distance. I ducked for cover. The air smelled of smoke. I opened my eyes and raised my head slowly.

Hank gestured to the plumes of gunk billowing over the parking lot. "Isn't that where I parked my car?"

I helped Hank fold up the blanket. Was there another hand in this? It could be just another disturbance in a succession of accidents. Maybe I was being paranoid, but I didn't think so.

By the time we reached the parking lot, fire trucks had arrived. I coughed from the debilitating smoke. The firemen dragged their hoses across the asphalt to the remains of Hank's wheels. The Edsel's hood lay on the ground at least ten feet from the rest of the charred frame and smoldering tires.

Hank approached a fireman who doused his pride and joy with water. "My Edsel, my beautiful Edsel."

The firemen shooed him away.

Hank retreated helplessly. "All the original parts, nothing Mexican or Chinese about these. I walked miles through fields, took trips to bone yards across America, paid a fucking fortune. Insurance will never cover this." He removed his baseball cap and held it over his heart. "Why do people hate us so much?"

The memory of Juanita's ammonia and fertilizer in her kitchen superimposed over his face. "What makes you think this is about you?"

Ignoring my question, he said, "We'd better call the Feds."

"What about the police?"

He wiped his brow with the back of his hand. "This is a government matter." Hank asked for my cell phone.

"Where's yours?"

"In my glove compartment with my latest copy of the *Scrape and Knuckles*."

CHAPTER 10

"SPEAK SOFTLY AND CARRY A SMARTPHONE."
-- The Matchmaker's Bible

I hitched a ride home with the sumo wrestler, unwilling to stick around for the Feds. Besides, the hunk knew where to find me, if he wanted to. I climbed inside Arnold's black pickup truck. The bench seat tilted like a seesaw and I landed against his thigh. Too bad he wasn't my type. I inched away from him, unable to develop enough traction until I grabbed the door handle. I peeked at Arnold wondering how many airplane tickets it would take to buy him off. At least one for each buttock. How many hamburgers? One trans-sexual client was costly enough for me.

Could a tax dodger have gotten even with Hank? I wasn't convinced. How would someone like Juanita know about an IRS picnic? Why would she bother to bomb his car and not mine? She didn't impress me as the type to pay much attention to the IRS. My chest constricted. Maybe it wasn't her. Maybe it was another person. Never mind it was a different MO. What was to prevent Fong's killer from changing methods? Call me paranoid. Call me a healthy skeptic. I took out my BlackBerry, clicked on Larry's stored number and nabbed him before he left the station. He could be a pain in the noogie. Still, he represented a cross between fuzz and extended family to me and I needed to talk, so I invited him over for a drinky-poo.

Larry arrived a couple of hours later, all apologies for having been held up on a call. The advantage to having a history with somebody was the familiarity it implied with his imperfections. The disadvantage was his knowledge of yours. Mr. Neat and Tidy surveyed my townhouse with an it's-getting-a-little-shabby-around-the-edges expression. Not that it was any of his business, but I saw the worn fabrics, paint marks and floor scratches with fresh eyes.

He sat down on the steps leading to the dining room. "Have you got any tomato juice?"

"You're still a vegetarian?"

"Yup."

From the size of his gut, he must have been eating a lot of mayonnaise on his tofu burgers lately.

He turned to Sweet Pea. "Give Daddy a kiss."

She licked his cheek and his face softened. She brought him her ball. Head lowered, tush in the air, she taunted him with it, until he tossed it across the room, narrowly missing my crystal lamp.

His gaze cut into mine. "She's getting a little gray around the whiskers."

"Aren't we all?"

He sighed. "I'm glad you called."

"I'm glad, too," I said, remembering my agenda.

I went into the kitchen, fetched a glass of water for him and dished out a package of soybeans. Since it was a mild evening, I suggested we move to the patio. I carried the soybeans outside and set it on a wrought-iron-and-glass table. Before we sat down, I brushed off the yellow sailcloth cushions with a napkin. Then I brought up Juanita Arroyo.

Larry interrupted me. "You won't have to worry about her anymore." He shook his head in dismay. "She blew herself up a couple of hours ago. Must have been looking for some free publicity."

"For Abu Syaar?"

He nodded. "I guess she thought it was good for business." His iPhone pinged. He lifted it out of his belt case, looked at his text message and returned it. Frowning, he said, "I've got to go."

"Wait just a minute."

He was out the door before I could ask more questions.

＝＋＝

Go figure female jihadists. I chewed on a soybean. Why would they want to blow themselves up? I doubted they were aiming for a bunch of male virgins when they were dead. What woman would want even one? I got in the car, turned on the radio and heard more of the story on the way to Hangar's cleaners. Juanita Arroyo had self-destructed at home. Surprising she hadn't chosen a federal building, instead of the corner of Vermont and Eighty-eighth Street to make a statement. Maybe she wasn't trying to make a statement. Could she have spilled some fertilizer on her cookies accidentally? The Feds were supposed to be sifting through the evidence, in search of a terrorist link. There was some speculation Abu Sayyar had planned to make room for a mosque six thousand miles from Mecca. What was wrong with the Isa Mosque a couple of blocks away from Juanita's house? The idea of Islamic factions getting along was as farfetched as Hamas and Israel making nice.

I picked up my dress for the American Cancer Society's cocktail party and silent auction, then drove to Eighty-eighth and Vermont. The intersection was barricaded because of the investigation at Juanita's house, so I parked a couple of blocks away and walked over. I could think of better places for an evening stroll. The air smelled of ashes, causing my chest to tighten. Again. Klieg lights crisscrossed the sky. I could see fire trucks, ambulances and cop cars in the distance. On second thought, this was probably one of the safest nights in the 'hood. I heard a sneeze and swiveled around.

The street lamp illuminated a tiny woman huddled against the post with a child, both of whom were filthy. I stood there rooted to the ground. The girl's eyes were as lively as Fong's. Was I hallucinating? The woman wasn't wearing a headscarf, and the short frizz blanketing her scalp looked as if it belonged to a person fresh out of chemotherapy. Could Larry have been wrong about Juanita? The Feds wouldn't release her name without positive identification or would they? We studied each other like a pair of wrestlers in the ring.

She hissed, "I warned those broads to be careful. They wouldn't listen."

"Juanita?" I stammered.

"Who else?"

"You're supposed to be dead."

"Am I?" she said dryly.

"What were you trying to do?"

"I stand by the Fifth Amendment." Juanita cackled. "Do you think I'll pass?"

"For what?"

"For a nurse in a hospital." She patted her head. "I never did like wearing a hijab. I feel so liberated." Her eyes narrowed. "I just hope the little fucker made the last insurance payment."

"Before you killed him?"

My question appeared to amuse her. "Next time, I'll have to hire a couple of shepherds who can read a map."

A silence stretched between us.

"Did your people blow up an Edsel today?"

"Wouldn't you like to know?"

"What does it take to get a straight answer out of you?" I waved an index finger at her. "With one call, I could have ten thousand cops here."

"Yeah?" She leered at me. "And one thousand'll be after you, too."

An ash landed on my cheek and I brushed it away. The Feds must have planted a false story about her death to lure her out of hiding. At least she was on the run, which ought to slow her down for awhile.

I crossed the street, racking my brain for another way to explore Fong's terrorist connections beside his widow. A crowd swarmed in front of the South L.A. barrier. I went around the block to the other side, in search of the best vantage point for a glimpse at the leveled house. Snatches of Spanish and English, baby's cries and shouts bombarded my ears. I squeezed past locals to the front of the line and saw where the roof had collapsed like a drunk in a truck-stop bar. One of the investigators with his back to me resembled the hunk. My heart knocked in my chest. When he turned sideways, his neck resembled a turkey's wattle. Oh, please. The hunk didn't have a wattle. Out of the corner of my eye, I spotted the man with a macaw on his shoulder. I elbowed my way over to him and stopped behind him. Either he or the bird--somebody--smelled like sawdust.

"Cute bird," I said.

"Say hello to Petey."

I leaned forward. "Hello, Petey."

"Twitter, twitter."

I did a double take. "Not tweet, tweet?"

"Twitter, twitter."

I sidled up to them. "What's with the bird?"

"He's got quite an ear." The man gazed at me with a mesmerized expression. "Hey, I remember you. You've been here before."

"Good memory."

"You sure pick some exciting times to come by."

I smiled in acknowledgement. "Glad you still have a place to live."

"Touch wood." The man tapped his turban.

Touch wood," the macaw echoed.

The man repositioned the bird on his forefinger. "Wonder what they were doing in there."

"Heard they were making bombs."

"You don't say." He chewed his lip.

I nodded. "How well did you know them?"

He said in a confidential tone, "Prefer to stick to myself, if you know what I mean."

"Twitter, twitter. Download twitter."

"Wait just a second. Is he trying to tell me something?"

The man rolled his shoulders. "We spend a lot of time together. Don't pay attention."

I stroked the bird's back, having no idea if Fong had been a member of Twitter or not. Why would I care about my janitor's tweets before his death? It was a different story now. I hiked back to my car, locked myself inside and fished out my BlackBerry. I logged on to the site and searched for Fong Arroyo, worried he might be using another name for a handle. Geronimo. I found him and scrolled through his tweets.

Up, dogs, up. Time for all dogs to get up. Coyotes, deer and foxes to chase. Up, dogs, up.

What dogs? Still, why would Fong incriminate him-self--in code or not--online, where nothing was sacred?

Here comes the promised rain. Drip, drip, drip, L.A.

More subterfuge?

The violet is my favorite flower. Violets look lovely in pots against buildings.

Wait. Violets *do* grow in pots. Maybe I was jumping to conclusions. I continued to navigate between his tweets and links. I learned he'd been following thirty-five tweeters and fifty-seven had been following him, which included his three children in the Philippines--a son who worked as a concierge at the Manila Hyatt, another who was a veterinarian (like father, like son?) and a third who grew orchids. Then a message flashed on the screen, telling me somebody named Snake Man was following me.

I tweeted, *Who's Snake Man?*

Slither, slither.

Do I know you?

Hisss.

Holy Christ. Who was this creep? I tried to pull up Snake Man's profile but couldn't find one. Too bad I wasn't privy to his Twitter password. I captured a screen shot and emailed it to the cops.

The cops neglected to get back to me before I left the house in the morning. I skipped breakfast and brought Sweet Pea to the vet for a bordetella booster shot. On the way to the office, I picked up an orange scone and cup of Starbucks French Roast decaf, which I downed at my desk. The scone was tangy and crunchy. Never mind the carbs. After my encounter with Snake Man on Twitter the night before, I craved some comfort food. My landline thrummed and so did my heart. I pressed the speakerphone button.

Lyons said in a slothful tone, "We've traced your tweeter to the main Santa Monica public library."

"Who is he?"

"Lots of luck."

"Don't they keep records on their computers?"

"Not for Wi-Fi."

"What about the security cameras?"

"Sorry, no snakes."

My first appointment wasn't until eleven. I slapped a sign on the door stating I'd be back in an hour and zipped over to Santa Monica's main library to have a first-hand look at the premises.

Santa Monica, once dubbed the people's republic because of its homeless population and stringent rent-control laws had become gentrified as fast as landlords could tear down apartment houses and build pricey condominiums.

I shot down Lincoln and cut over to Seventh Street, where I parked underground and came up to the entrance. A commercial mobile hung from the lobby's ceiling urging patrons to be creative with their library. How creative could I be in identifying a face-less wonder?

Sunshine spilled in from the floor-to-ceiling windows. Snake Man could be any one of the derelicts, retirees, or bookworms orbiting through the rooms or none of the above. Take your pick. I roamed past an unmanned information desk and graphic-novels display and stepped upstairs to the computer section open to the public. I sauntered over to a terminal, where a man in a red shirt sat glued to a screen featuring a recipe for killer short ribs. I leaned over his shoulder and suggested more hot sauce.

"You think so?"

"Definitely."

A woman beside Red Shirt filled out an online job application for Disney Studios. Based on her tan, she had been out of work for a while. I parked myself next to her. To blend in, I sent off a reminder for my upcoming Hawaiian mixer. I felt someone breathing down my neck and gave a look.

A man with fetid breath said, "How long you gonna be, lady?" We're on the honor s-s-system, you know."

The beanie on his head accentuated a pair of Alfred E. Neuman ears. Since the other terminals were still in use, I picked myself up, feeling generous, so he could have a seat. Without so much as a thank you, he exchanged places with me and began to Google snakes. Holy bananas. Was he trying to tell me something? I didn't bother to ask. I scooted downstairs to the first floor and out the door and got in touch with Lyons.

He said, "Wait a minute. Is the man about five feet, eight?"

"Yup."

"Is he wearing a gold beanie?"

"That's him."

"He's one of ours."

I returned to the office feeling sheepish. To distract myself, I combed through the current matchmaker ads in print. When I turned to page twenty-four of *Angelino Magazine*, I spotted Polly's spread beside a Rolex advertisement. I stared at the couple sipping champagne on a bridge in the photo and my stomach quavered. How dare she steal my March layout? I picked up the phone to give her a piece of my mind.

"What the hell do you think you're doing, Polly? Can't you get your own ideas?"

She said in an icy tone, "I don't know what you're talking about."

"My copy, my concept in *Angelino Magazine*. You'd better not pull the same stunt next month."

"You'll be lucky if you're still around next month."

"Don't be so sure, you plagiarizing bitch." I slammed down the phone feeling the vibration in my arm.

I reached for my decaf, resolved to survive, and cradled the coffee cup in my hands. In truth, I was hanging on by my fingernails. My business plan had taken into consideration the slow times but not murder. I had to find Fong's killer pronto.

Alexis showed up looking like Lucy on steroids in a bright red wig.

"Well, well, well. When did you get sprung?"

"Boy, am I glad to be out of there. Jails are not for ladies, my dear."

"I suppose the same could be said for gentlemen."

She gravitated to my love seat and slouched in it with one leg under the other. "I tried to go to work this morning. They didn't want me around. Can you imagine?" A hurt expression flitted through her eyes. "They wouldn't even let me clean out my desk. What am I, a Pollyanna?"

I set down my cup. "You mean pariah."

"Pollyanna, pariah--What's the big deal?" She extricated herself from the cushions and strutted over to me. "They have no right to keep my patent diary from me."

"Don't you have another copy?"

She said in a condescending voice, "I can't very well register it without proof in my own handwriting."

"Pardon my ignorance." I paused. "Can't they FedEx it to you?"

"You think I intend to risk something so valuable getting lost?"

I leaned back, gripping the edge of my desk. "Isn't that what tracking numbers are for?"

Alexis unsnapped her handbag, ripped out a nylon cord with a plastic rectangle suspended from it and slung the thing over my head.

"Alexis, what are you doing?"

She smiled an enthusiastic smile. "This will get you in the door. They never look at the picture. It's a five-by-eight, black and white journal that I keep in my bottom desk drawer."

I rubbed my temples feeling a headache coming on. "Break-ins are hard to explain to the cops."

"It's going to be worth a lot of money once we--"

"What's this *we* business?"

She made a grandiose gesture. "Have you no mercy for a person who just posted her house and twenty percent of her assets for bail? With your blonde hair...if you stand up very straight and tall..."

I gazed at her in disbelief. "You're serious, aren't you?"

"Of course, I'm serious." She produced a hand-drawn map of the building and slapped it in my palm.

I paused. "Don't you have any other friends?"

"But you're the only one I trust."

"How did I get so lucky?" I returned the map and badge to her. "Has somebody who goes by the name of Snake Man gotten in touch with you?"

"No. Why?"

"What did you tell Fong about your new generation of bomb?"

"What do you mean?"

I said in a tight voice, "I regret having to tell you this, Alexis. Fong wasn't as innocent as I thought." I swallowed hard. "You've heard about Abu Sayyar..."

"He was a member?"

"There's a very good chance."

"No lie."

I nodded. "Yup."

Alexis broke into a shit-faced grin. "Now you have to do it."

———※ ※———

What was I getting myself into? Could Alexis Grand's diary have something to do with Fong's murder? Don't go there. Not on your life. Stop. But when I passed the Krispy Kreme doughnut shop on the corner, I had a sudden impulse to know.

CHAPTER 11

"IF YOU THINK IT'S TOO GOOD TO BE TRUE, IT PROBABLY IS."

-- *The Matchmaker's Bible*

Neutronics Research and Development was a sprawling converted Pasadena warehouse just off the Arroyo Secco Parkway, not far from my favorite Trader Joe's. To discourage unwanted visitors, it had no sign, just an address on the building.

If anyone questioned me about my intentions, what would I say? I was running a special offer for geniuses making over one hundred K annually. But how would I explain being caught red-handed with Alexis' ID? Insanity, it had to be that. If I copped an insanity plea, how could they not believe me?

I shut off the ignition and consulted Alexis' map. Her office was supposed to be on the second floor. I refolded the map, stuffed it in my purse, slid out of the car and buttoned my blazer. A bowlegged security guard was alone at the entrance. I took a breath and felt my lungs constrict. The burning in my chest was probably from the bad air. Then again, it could be from fear. I placed my thumb over Alexis' picture and forged ahead.

I nonchalantly approached the bow-legged security guard at the entrance. He whisked Alexis' badge from my hand and flipped it over, picture side up. Holy chakras.

"I didn't always look like this," I said, trying to distract him.

He said with an approving smile, "You look fine to me."

I searched his background face for an indication of insincerity but couldn't find it.

"Yeah, yeah, yeah." I played along with him.

He cocked his head to the side. "I only say it to the pretty ones."

I thanked him with a demure smile.

He returned Alexis' badge to me and waved me inside. At any moment, I expected to be busted, but it was too late to bail now. I traipsed through the front door and glanced back at the guard. His reflection in the window indicated he remained at the entrance. I continued down the corridor, noting the security cameras in place.

Alexis had warned me about the zigzag nature of the cubicles. I attempted to fit in on my way past some of the employees. A couple of Lakers fans at the water cooler were discussing the previous night's loss. I found the closest elevator, which had a sign on the door announcing an afternoon ice cream party in the cafeteria. I liked ice cream all right. If I stuck around for Chunky Monkey, I might learn something. If I stuck around long enough for Chunky Monkey, I stood a good chance of getting arrested. Better not push it. I caught the elevator and rode up with a voluptuous brunette, who filled the air with a pleasant vanilla aroma. She was just Roger's type. Too bad I had more important priorities at the moment. She gazed at me with a curious expression. I smiled a casual smile.

The brunette appeared to be searching for the right words. "Hey, you look familiar."

My smile wilted.

"I know who you are."

I heard myself say, "You do?"

"You're *her* friend."

"Whose?"

"What's her name? The woman match on TV..." As she reached for my identification badge, I pulled away quickly, breaking into a sweat at my flop performance.

Her eyes narrowed. "Just a minute...That woman who won the Quick Pick last week...t*hat's* who you are."

I exhaled casting my gaze on her nude pumps.

She said, "So what are you going to do with all that money?"

"This is my last week." I neglected to add, my last half hour before Soledad.

A ping announced the second floor. I scurried out of the elevator and glanced back. The woman hadn't gotten out. My blouse stuck to my skin like peanut butter. Having no idea which way to go, I barreled past a conference room and laboratory, in which a man with hairy arms fiddled with a circuit board. It was too risky to ask him for directions, or attempt to consult the map again, so I wandered vaguely through the halls. I passed a series of offices, rounded a corner and came upon a door with Alexis Grand's name on it. My heart did a two-step. No one was around. I let myself in and shut the door behind me.

A vertical window afforded a narrow view of the outside world, not unlike Alexis' tunnel vision. The room smelled like rancid coffee, originating from a mug on her desk stamped with a Norman Rockwell design. An empty rectangle defined the space where her computer must have been. Anxious to make it snappy, I opened the bottom drawer, where her patent diary was supposed to be. I came upon a hand mirror, hairbrush and bottle of shocking pink nail polish, but no black and white journal. There was something else behind a partition--round, firm and rubbery. I pulled it out slowly. A dildo. My, my, my, far be it for me to tell a person how to spend her coffee breaks. I tried to shut the drawer. A wad of paper prevented it from closing. I tugged, until it tore loose and then quickly pieced together the parts. On closer inspection, it was a catalogue entitled *Exotic Animals*. The label bore Alexis Grand's name. Someone had removed an order form from inside the booklet. The back cover gave an Iowa post office box and toll-free number. I stashed the catalogue in my purse, anxious for an explanation.

⇐ ⇒

I hotfooted it to my car. Aware of somebody behind me, I didn't turn around. I picked up my pace, expecting to be surrounded at any minute by a cadre of security guards. A familiar voice called out my name. I gave a look over my shoulder. Hank Buyers waved at me, beaming his happy juice smile.

I slapped my chest in surprise, almost glad to see him, given the alternative. "What are you doing here?"

"You didn't answer my calls, so I followed you." Hank's jaw tightened. "In that rented piece of crap." He gestured to the parking lot.

I stood there in silence, staring at his baldhead. "I really have to go," I heard myself babble.

"Just tell me one thing. How did you know there was a bomb under my hood?"

"I didn't," I said, having visions of cameras zooming in on us.

"So I think I can get that file back from Arnold. Would you like to have dinner some time?"

"Let's talk later," I said in a rapid cadence.

I fled to my car and took off, relieved to be out of there. Trembling, I tried Alexis's landline. Her machine picked up and I left a message.

By the time I arrived at my office, I hadn't heard from Alexis. Only my eleven o'clock had called to reschedule. I made myself a cup of decaf.

Nathan, a producer with a lower case *p*, since he had yet to produce anything, had slipped some new photos of himself through my mail slot. I set them aside and settled into my swivel chair with my decaf and the catalogue. After I taped it back together, I called the toll-free number listed on the back page.

A computer voice said, "Our menu has changed. To continue in English, press one, en espanol, numero dos."

I made my selection.

"Press one for monitors, two for venomous snakes, three for constrictors, four for live mice, chickens, rats and mealworms. If you've been bitten by any of our exotic animals, hang up immediately and dial 911."

Unless you want to commit suicide, I thought. I chose option three.

"May I help you?" a woman said with a Midwestern twang.

"My python arrived dead."

"Are you sure?"

"I ought to know a dead one from a live one."

"When did you receive it?"

I hesitated. "Two weeks ago."

"Out of warranty."

My voice softened. "I would have been in touch sooner. I had another death."

"What did you say your name was?"

"Alexis Grand."

She said with a suspicious edge, "Alexis Grand?"

I chortled. "Had you there for a minute."

Silence.

"One moment, please."

Another silence before the rep returned to the line. "Don't have any record of you. Could it be under another name?"

"Try Alexander, or Alex."

"Are you sure we sold it to you?"

"It says right here on the box..."

"Do you have your receipt?"

"Sorry, I can't find it."

"I can't help you, lady."

I clicked off the phone, puzzled. Had Alexis used a pseudonym to purchase a snake? If she didn't, what was the point of her keeping an *Exotic Animals* catalogue in her drawer? I tried to peel back the label to see if there was another addressee underneath it. The paper disintegrated in my hands. A woman burst into my office reeking of nicotine. I shoved it in my file cabinet and shut the drawer.

"Millie Gillespie," the woman said in a smoker's rasp. She handed me a business card with the words BAIL BONDS INSURANCE SPECIALIST under her name. "Where's Alexis Grand?"

"I have no idea." I gulped down the rest of my rancid-tasting decaf.

"You're her friend?"

"Who told you that?"

"A little birdie, a jail birdie." Her tone turned from mocking to gruff. "I think the broad skipped." She adjusted the skirt of her navy blue suit, emphasizing her pear-shaped figure with ample hips.

"That's highly unlikely."

"How do you know?"

"For one thing, she just sent me on an errand."

"What kind of errand?" She coughed a phlegmy cough.

"None of your business."

"Yeah, well, she's in deep doo-doo, I don't mind telling you."

"I doubt she'd forfeit--"

"Yeah?" Millie snickered. "That's what they all say. When you've been in this business as long as I have, they're never gonna, but they do. If you hear from her, tell her she missed a court appearance this afternoon." She started for the door and shot a dubious look at me. "So tell me, are you good at this?"

"Good at what?"

"You know, good at what you do. Haven't had a date in ten years." She took off her jacket and draped it over her arm, revealing a Calvin Klein label in the lining. "I love beards," she gushed. "The Freud type, if you know what I mean."

I studied her a moment. She had nice features and exuded a no-nonsense manner. I told her about Zach and handed her a By Invitation Only brochure with an application inside. There was somebody for everybody-- well, almost everybody.

CHAPTER 12

"BE CAREFUL OF SECOND-GUESSING CHEMISTRY."

-- The Matchmaker's Bible

To kill the smoke aroma in my office, I spritzed the air with Lysol and tossed the canister in my desk. Why did Alexis send me to find her patent diary, if she planned to skip out on me? As a matchmaker, I prided myself on my ability to read people, to get into their skin. It just didn't make sense. She struck me as self-indulgent, naïve, outrageous, at times, but never one to sacrifice her house and future by choice.

My thoughts strayed to her dog, Puppy. Doubting Alexis would leave him alone, unless she planned to return shortly, I decided to spin by her Brentwood home to stake out the premises.

I slung my purse over my shoulder and strode into the lobby. Zach slipped through the front door, looking as if he had died and didn't know it.

"What's the matter?"

"That terrorist on the news, Juanita Arroyo--you've heard of her?"

I nodded.

"She just tried to sell me a couple of bomb-making manuals. Don't ask me why. "Isn't she supposed to be dead?"

I fessed up to my recent sightings of her.

"Can you imagine? The crazy bitch attempted to get me to start an anarchy section next to my sci-fi. She claimed it would be good for business. I hurried her out so fast--"

"Did you call the cops?"

"Let somebody else be the Good Samaritan."

"I know what you mean." I deposited my purse on the reception desk and gestured to a chair. "Have a seat."

He hesitated. "I'm on my way to yoga across the street. I just had to tell somebody. Don't let me keep you."

"That's okay. One of my clients has disappeared. It's probably a misunderstanding."

"Do I know the person?"

"You almost met her--Alexis Grand."

"No lie." He slid down into the Lotus position on the carpet and engaged in some deep breathing. Legs folded, palms upright, he was the poster boy for Prozac pesto. I gazed at the neon yoga sign across the street, feeling the need for a new mantra myself.

"I was just about to call you," I fibbed, guilty over the way I'd been neglecting my work. "Did you speak to my flight attendant?"

"Ruths are bad luck."

"Don't tell me your superstitious."

"How about a Chloe?" he said with a seductive smile.

"Trust me. You and Ruth--"

His smile faded. "I don't want any Ruths."

"Even a Baby Ruth?"

His good humor returned.

My thoughts turned to Millie Gillespie. Although she appeared to be more of a realist and tougher sell than Ruth, the old black magic was as good a way as any to account for chemistry. I floated her name past Zach. Never mind he didn't have a beard. He could grow one. Besides, Millie hadn't returned her application yet and I needed the business.

Zach smiled a wan smile. "How's her voice?"

"I'd say it's in the contralto range."

"That sounds like Alexis'."

"She's her skip tracer."

He wiggled his eyebrows. "Handcuffs?"

"Pairs of them, walls of them, cats of nine tails."

"Right on."

After Zach departed for his yoga class across the street, I contacted Millie, told her about him and urged her to send me a check ASAP.

Twenty minutes later, I showed up in Alexis' driveway. Somebody had removed the crime tape from the house. Was her car still in the garage? I couldn't tell from the street. What about Puppy? I circled the property, listening for evidence of a dog. The only barking sounded far away. I sauntered up to the door. Several newspapers had accumulated on the porch, which I scooped up. The house was quiet. I rang the bell, giving rise to chimes. I waited a couple of moments. No response, then swung around to the back and peeked over the fence. Her yard contained dog poop, the ashen color of which indicated it had been there for a while. But there was no dog. I returned to the entrance, wishing I had a key. I fumbled for one under the mat and in the planters. No such luck. I went next door and knocked.

"I'm not interested in selling," a woman said as she peered through the peephole of her gray Craftsman.

"Unless you can beat the two-point-four mil they got next door by ten percent."

"You have it all wrong, lady. I'm a friend of Alexis Grand."

"Don't know her and don't care to." She shut the flap in my face.

A Buick Skylark backed out of a driveway on the opposite side of Alexis' house.

"Excuse me," I said, flagging down the driver.

The old man braked.

I trotted over to him with a smile. "When was the last time you saw Alexis Grand?"

His rheumy eyes expressed confusion. "The wife's been in the hospital."

"Sorry to hear it."

He shook his head. "Gallbladder. I thought they took it out a while ago. How many do you have? A wonderful neighbor that Alexis, helpful and strong, really strong. You should see the way she carries in a sofa bed."

"Do you happen to have a key to her place?"

He shook his head.

I glanced back at Alexis' house. The front windows were closed. I spotted an ADT sign on the lawn, indicating she had an armed security system, which I presumed was on. I checked the side gate. Padlocked. I tugged on the tumbler. It didn't budge. I had never picked a lock before, but remembered Larry using his

MasterCard to jimmy ours after we locked ourselves out one fine afternoon. Thirteen years of marriage to a cop ought to have taught me something. Within the last twenty-four hours, I had staged a break-in because of Alexis Grand and now contemplated another one, thanks to her. Although she was hardly my favorite person, she had become a life-altering experience.

I spun around to the alley. A tall hedge blocked my view of her backyard. I returned to the car, plucked a pair of rubber gloves from my emergency tool kit in the trunk and strode over to the front entrance. If I set off her alarm, what would happen? How many years would I get for breaking and entering? My heart sputtered like a motor. I lifted the Visa out of my wallet.

A mailman completed his route across the street and hopped into his truck. I grabbed hold of the doorknob and slipped my Visa into the jamb. It didn't fit. My hands tingled. I rotated the card, but it still didn't work. To commemorate our third anniversary, Larry had given me a set of picks. Miffed at the impersonal nature of his gift, I had thrown them back at him. Damn. I could use them now. I shuffled through the rest of my cards. The ATM said, DO NOT USE TO OPEN DOORS, OR IT WILL INVALIDATE THE CARD. The others were either too flimsy or thick. The ATM was my best shot. The last time I looked, I had nineteen dollars and ninety-nine cents in my bank account. That was after the twenty-two-dollar expenditure for Girl Scout cookies. I hoped jimmying a lock wouldn't destroy my debit card, but what difference did it make? I was under the forty-dollar limit for another withdrawal. I inserted it in the crease and it snapped.   Holy Mother of God. My Vons card could withstand three swipes and the Costco one six without breaking. I kicked the door in frustration and it sprang open. Go figure. If only I had checked the handle first, I could have saved myself a lot of aggravation. So I wasn't perfect. No kidding. I was susceptible to the occasional lapse in judgment.

The house felt cool. I glanced at the mail surrounding my feet. It consisted of an advertisement for a party store, a couple of bank statements and a two for one coupon for Fredrick's of Hollywood crotchless panties. Buy one. Get the second pair free.

"Alexis...Alexis, are you there?"

Nobody answered. I snatched up the mail and stole through the living and dining rooms with it. The floorboards creaked underfoot. I reached the kitchen, which smelled like yesterday's garbage.

A bowl of soggy Cheerios and carton of milk rested on the granite island next to the Yellow Pages opened to the "Cs". What could the guidewords COSMETICS-COSTUMES possibly mean?   Everything Alexis wore resembled a costume. I hit the redial button on her kitchen cordless. A receptionist for Solutions Skin Care answered. I learned Alexis had an eleven-fifteen

Restylane appointment with the dermatologist on Friday, which she hadn't cancelled. Would she show up? I left a message with the receptionist for Alexis to call me. I sniffed the milk carton on the island. Its contents didn't smell sour, so she couldn't have been gone long. Alexis must have disappeared some time after breakfast but before the mail arrived.

I proceeded to the master bedroom. Recalling Fong's lifeless body under the shawl, I gathered up my mojo and marched inside. No one was there. The filtered light from the plantation shutters revealed a pair of black ostrich slippers on the carpet and three wig stands across the dresser. A mass of frosted curls cascaded over one of the Styrofoam forms and a straight champagne-blonde mane over another, but the third was bare. (Alexis must have been wearing her Lucy version.) A towel that was a relic from an old Obama-Biden campaign sprawled across the dressing room floor.

This didn't strike me as the home of somebody who had run away or been abducted. I continued through a short hall, past the office and guest bedroom, to the attached garage. Her car wasn't there. I retraced my steps and heard a noise coming from the front of the house. I ducked into a closet and stood there with my ear against the jamb.

A pair of shoes slapped the floor, which probably belonged to Alexis, a cop or the murderer. Drawers scraped on their hinges. Silence. In the darkness, I flicked on my cell phone. The backlight enabled me to find Alexis' phone number among my contacts. I called it and waited for somebody to answer. Her machine picked up. I hung up. The footsteps intensified. I grabbed a hanger and lifted my purse, ready to attack. There was another silence. Somebody was wearing perfume, a lilac scent I didn't recognize. I tried to stop myself from sneezing, but I couldn't control my nose.

"Who's there?" a man said. His voice didn't fit with the fragrance.

I thrust open the door.

The man jumped back, shielding his face with tattooed arms. "I can explain everything. Please don't tell." He lowered his arms to the sides of a floral housedress. "If the people at Wanda's Cleaning Service find out I've been running around in drag..." His eyes leaked tears. "It's not easy getting a job these days with a PhD in classics."

I heard myself say, "Who are you? Where's Alexis?"

"How am I supposed to know? She called and told me to pick up my check." His eyes darted around the hall. "Did you happen to see one lying around?"

"She called you?"

He shrugged. "Somebody did."

"When?"

"Yesterday."

"What else did she say?"

"That she wouldn't be needing me for awhile."

"Why?"

"You got me."

"Did she mention where she was?"

"I didn't ask."

Why bother to tell your maid to pick up a check if you're on the run? The cross-dresser beat it. I went to the window, peeked through the curtains and saw him shove a motorcycle helmet on his head, pair of goggles over his eyes and roar away on his bike. What was wrong with this picture?

I pulled out my BlackBerry and contacted Wanda's Cleaning Service to verify his story. Sure enough, the company had no idea who he was, or what he was doing here. The receptionist was quick to add, the agency's policy was to bill and collect from its clients directly, confirming my reservations about the man in the housedress.

Given his getup, he could be one of Alexis' friends. I didn't catch his name. According to Alexis, her patent diary was worth a hell of a lot more than a cleaning gig. She'd sent me to find it, which had led to an *Exotic Animals* catalogue and a cross-dresser, who appeared to be up to no good. Who was this guy?.

H hustled to my car. Rain began to fall and the air smelled dank. My mood darkened like the sky. I climbed inside and turned on my windshield wipers.

By the time I reached my office, a number of fires had broken out. There was a message from an irate client, whom I had matched with the same man twice by mistake, another from Hank Buyers and a third from my landlord, informing me I'd forgotten to pay the rent. I had to do a better job of keeping my affairs straight. I opened a drawer to remove my checkbook and saw something brown with stripes that looked like a necktie display at Macy's. The drawer bounced a little.

A snake.

CHAPTER 13

"TRUST YOUR INTUITION."
-- *The Matchmaker's Bible*

I shut the drawer, bolted out of there and slammed the door behind me. Was it a boa like the one wrapped around Fong's torso? I didn't look too hard. When I saw its flat glassy stare and tongue move toward me, I was finished, demolished, kaput. I rushed outside and called the cops.

Madeline showed up on my doorstep with Jason. "About Brian--he seems to be avoiding me."

"This is not a good time," I managed to say. "There's a snake in my office."

"Maybe we could get it a flute," Jason said.

I gave him a menacing look and he cowered.

"Did you notice anyone lurking around?"

Jason nodded. "There was this man."

"What man?"

Madeleine winked at me. "You know how he is about men. Let's go, Jason." She yanked him away.

I stood there a moment trying to compose myself, then tore into Paradise Yacht Tours next door in search of a witness. I found Ishmael cozying up to my competitor, Polly, at his desk.

"What are *you* doing here, Polly?"

"Too bad you're not his type," she said in a haughty voice.

"What's that? Bitchy?"

"Scratch, scratch, claw, claw." She pawed the air like a cat.

"Did you put a snake in my drawer?"

"I don't know what you're talking about."

"I wouldn't be surprised after the way you ripped off my ad."

"Are you out of your mind?"

Was she trying to force me out of business? Could Polly and Ishmael be in cahoots? I had so many conflicting thoughts I didn't know what to believe. Her leopard-print scarf framed a face with pinched features.

I shifted my gaze from her to Ishmael. "Did either of you hear any noise in my office this afternoon?"

Caressing Ishmael's hairy arm, she said, "Don't you think we have better things to do with our time? We were just negotiating a sunset cruise."

"I hope somebody else drives the boat." I paused. "Did he tell you he gets seasick?"

Ishmael sighed. "I really ought to be in the Land Rover business."

I became aware of footsteps outside, lost interest in the captain and his catch and thrust open the door. Lyons lingered under the overhang with a couple of boys in blue.

"You're a comforting sight. Where's your partner?"

The corners of his mouth hinted of a smile. "He's taking care of some paperwork in the car. You know how he is about snakes."

Lyons' halo of silver hair framed a craggy face that alternated between attractive and unattractive depending on the angle, any of which might have appealed to Alexis, if she were here.

I led them into my office, catching a whiff of wintergreen from one of the boys in blue. The other gave his knuckles a loud crack. I followed them around the lobby while they looked for clues.

Lyons stopped in front of my photo gallery. "These are your clients?"

"Would you like a list?"

He nodded. "Which of them met Fong Arroyo?"

I assured him Fong's introduction to Alexis was a one-shot deal.

Lyons peered at me through slits. "Did anyone see a person hanging around with a snake?"

"I wouldn't know," I said, neglecting to mention Madeleine's son, Jason, who couldn't be trusted.

Lyons directed the two officers with him to sniff around the premises. After they were gone, he concluded there was no evidence of forced entry. He shifted feet. "Who else beside you has a key?"

"Maybe the new janitor."

"Have you met the person?"

"Not yet."

"Did you leave your door open?"

"I always lock it."

"How about a window?"

I lifted my shoulders. "I wouldn't swear to it."

"Is anything missing?"

"I didn't notice."

"Where's the snake?"

Reluctantly, I let him into my personal office, where the thing had pushed itself out of the drawer. It hissed at us and we stepped back.

Lyons said with a mesmerized expression, "It looks like another boa."

"A hungry one that would squeeze the life out of me, if given a chance."

"Do you have any idea who put it here?"

I thrust my hands in the air. Keeping my attention on the snake, I came clean about how Alexis had asked me to retrieve her patent diary from Neutronics R/D, and I had found an *Exotic Animals* catalogue addressed to her instead. I started to fetch the catalogue from my file cabinet.

Lyons barked at me. "Don't touch anything."

I cranked my body around, startled by his sudden authoritative tone.

"Let me get this straight." He eyed me with skepticism. "Alexis sent you to find a patent diary after they wouldn't let her back in." His tone climbed, as though he were asking a question. "But they let you in."

"Yes. Do you happen to know where it is?"

"I wish you'd leave the detective work to us and stick to your matchmaking." He tilted his head to the side.

Under the circumstances, I decided against bringing up Alexis' bank and credit card statements in my purse.

Someone rapped on the door.

"Enter at your own risk," I said, expecting another tenant, client or more cops.

I felt something on my legs and feared Lyons might be getting fresh with me.

"Don't move," he said, whipping out his gun.

I looked down at my legs and realized the snake had looped itself around them. It was a painful sucker.

"Holy ouch," I stammered. "Down, boy."

Zach appeared in the doorway, smiling. "What's a boa doing here?"

"How'd you know it's a boa?"

His smile evaporated. "There was this program about them on the Discovery Channel." He grabbed my umbrella from a stand near the door and pounded the carpet with it.

"Snakes are deaf," Lyons said.

"They respond to vibration."

"Who the hell are you?"

"I'm her client." Zach volunteered his business card, which Lyons snatched from him.

The snake started to unravel itself from my legs. Relieved, I watched it crawl toward the umbrella. The thing wrapped itself around the umbrella, which sprang open. Zach let go of the handle. The creature began to ingest it, apparently hungry. I heard foot-falls and looked up. The petite woman from Animal Control arrived with more gummy bears and another burlap sack to bag it.

I thanked Zach for his help.

He gazed at my legs. "You have a nasty bruise there. That sucker has muscles. It could have broken a bone."

I rubbed my painful shins. Someone clearly had access to my office. What else? I managed to dispel a clumsy threat this time, but what next, a poison break-fast burrito?

Zach said, "Hey, I haven't been able to get hold of Millie Gillespie. Will you check it out?"

"If she doesn't want you, I'll take you," I said in jest.

⟫⟪

I hobbled into the house, grabbed a couple of packages of frozen blueberries and flopped on the couch with them. Sweet Pea jumped into my lap and licked my face. Melt, melt. Zach had managed to save the day. Millie could do a lot worse than him. I retrieved my cell phone from my purse, left a message for her and marked it urgent. The blueberries began to feel heavy on my shins. I repositioned them on my legs and ferreted out Alexis' Wells Fargo and MasterCard statements. I tore open her credit card statement first. Holy cow. For a person who believed in paying cash, Alexis had made a lot of purchases with plastic during the month. She charged gasoline, groceries, prescriptions, dinners, a dress and a Robert Coin bracelet.

I ripped open her bank statement and studied her transactions. Wait. She managed to rack up one hundred forty dollars in bounced-check penalties. How could a research physicist be such a deadbeat with her finances? She began the statement period with a two-thousand-dollar surplus. On March fifth, she'd deposited six thousand clams, on March seventh, another twenty-five hundred. She wrote checks for eight grand to the IRS and fifteen hundred to the Franchise Tax Board. Both had cleared before the closing period. At least she believed in paying her taxes, unlike Mother. I zeroed in on a rubber check for fifty-three dollars and eighty-three cents, made payable to Madhatter's Costume and Beauty Supply, dated March tenth. Come to think of it, the Yellow Pages in her house were open to the guidewords COSMETICS–COSTUMES. Was there a connection? I cast aside the frozen blueberries on my legs. It was worth a shot in the dusk.

⇌ ⇌

Construction reduced Highland to two lanes. The man in back of me leaned on his horn. A teenager on my left extended his middle finger. I took road rage in stride, as long as it stopped short of semi-automatics. I turned on the radio. Another car chase wended its way through Culver City, shutting down the surrounding streets and providing the evening's entertainment. The real suspense rested with whether it would end in a crash or shootout, since no one ever got away. My thoughts strayed to Alexis, whose whereabouts were less clear. As the pop drama ended on some poor soul's lawn, I arrived at the corner of Hollywood and Vine. Madhatter's Costume Shop occupied a spot on the Hollywood Walk of Fame between the Dolby and Grauman Chinese Theatres. I made a left and parked on a side street.

From there, I joined hookers, tourists and movie-goers swirling through the streets with celebrity names and terrazzo-and-brass stars embedded in the pavement. Carried along by the bright lights and energy, I floated over to Madhatter's. I peeked in the window. The Little Bo Peep costume on display constituted a once-a-year statement for most but everyday fashion for Alexis. I surged through the door, and an impressive selection of wigs—some with sequins, others with beads and feathers—lured me to them. Could this be where she bought her wigs? I couldn't resist trying on a peacock blue number with acid green, neon pink and yellow highlights. All I needed was a rhinestone in my navel to complete the alternative look. My head felt as if it were in a compression chamber. How did Alexis do it? I peeled off the showstopper and marched over to a person wearing a caveman mask.

"Do you remember seeing this woman in here?" I showed him Alexis' picture and stared at him.

He grunted like a Neanderthal.

"Get real," I said.

"You a cop or something?"

"Just a friend."

He folded his arms. "Don't remember."

"You'd remember seeing this one." I eyed the masks of Marilyn, Elvis and Sir Paul on the wall behind him.

"What if I do?"

I produced proof of the returned check on Alexis' bank statement. "Can you tell me what this was for?"

"Why? Are you planning to pay up?"

"Maybe."

He removed his rubber disguise. I tried to decide whether it was an improvement or not but couldn't make up my mind.

He studied Alexis' bank statement a couple of beats, then went over to a computer and punched some keys.

"Oh, yeah." He wiggled his fingers.

"Excuse me?"

"The Scissorhands one."

"The Scissorhands?"

He nodded. "One of my favs."

It had been years since I had seen the movie *Edward Scissorhands*. Why would Alexis choose an androgynous supernatural character named Edward after becoming a woman? Once a geek, always a geek. What kind of scissors? Pinking shears, gardening, steal, or plastic. Where was the match? Paper, hair, human beings? From now on, I vowed to recruit only church-going, college-educated ladies and gentlemen without sexual confusion.

"I just love this job," he said. "One day, I can be Dracula. Ha, ha. The next, Richard Nixon." He held up two fingers. "I want to make it perfectly clear. Ha, ha."

His tattoos and piercings gave him the air of a run-away kid, instead of an United States president.

"Did she come in with anybody?"

He nodded. Toying with his mask, he said, "Some dude wearing a cobra thingy with a tail."

CHAPTER 14

"BE CAREFUL OF SNAKES WANDERING THROUGH THE GRASS."

-- The Matchmaker's Bible

Who was this cobra thingy with a tail? What would motivate Alexis to go off with a man dressed like a snake? The image of the Wanda's Cleaning Service imposter scooted through my consciousness. I wouldn't mind checking out his closet. My BlackBerry announced a call.

"Hey, I've been trying to reach you," said Larry. "Don't you listen to your voice mail? It's the LAPD annual fundraiser Saturday night and my date has the flu. Would you mind filling in for her?"

I quipped, "That was the trouble. I was always in second place."

"Don't tell me you're still on that kick. C'mon, I need help with the door prizes."

"And I need some help finding somebody wearing a snake costume." I briefed him on my conversation with the kid in the caveman's mask.

"Lyons and Garcia ought to be at the shindig."

"Are you trying to bribe me?"

"Would I do a thing like that?"

I attempted to wash away the memory of snakes with a long hot shower. Lots of luck. I marched over to the sink. In the mirror, I was as pale as Edward Scissorhands. At least I didn't have his scarred face. Never mind a few wrinkles. I couldn't remember the exact details of the movie, only that Edward had been shunned by society and forced to survive on his own. My thoughts segued to Alexis. I wondered if her disappearance was a case of life imitating art. Curious about whether my new follower was the real deal, I fished out my cell phone and logged on to to my Twitter account.

I tweeted, *I'm looking for Alexis Grand, last seen with a man in a cobra mask.*

Snake Man shot back, *Be careful, or you're next.*

Yikes.

Have we met?

Yesssss.

Refresh my memory.

Hisss.

Holy mortal alien. After my last fiasco with the cops, I didn't bother to capture another screen shot. I consulted my watch. The library closed in less than forty minutes. The chances of Snake Man being there were as unlikely as my developing another nostril, yet I threw on a pair of leggings and hoodie and made for the car.

I buckled up and spun out of the garage. How would I recognize him? He claimed to know me. Did I know him? A tattooed man in drag ought to be easy to spot. Likewise some fruitcake wearing a cobra mask. I should be so lucky. I sped down Culver Boulevard to Lincoln. My view changed from a dark artery to unsightly billboards, a bar featuring turtle races, a Harley store and vintage car dealership. I hurtled north, past the 10 Freeway, hung a left on Santa Monica Boulevard and shot into a space across from the main branch of the Santa Monica library. I jumped out of the car with my purse. The meter was one of those 24/7 jobs. Leave it to the city to rake in the revenue. I rummaged through my wallet for quarters. Damn. I was out of change. With my credit cards overextended, I decided to take my chances and risk a ticket. I bolted inside and almost collided with the security guard on duty.

Just past the circulation desk, I ran into Zach going the opposite way and did a stutter step. "What are you doing here?"

He said with a frown, "My computer's down. I have to register for the San Diego sci-fi conference by the end of today."

I rushed past him.

"What's the hurry?" he asked.

I neglected to answer.

He followed me to the computer section, which was empty, except for an unkempt woman who slept with her mouth open in front of one of the terminals.

I shook the woman. "Wake up. Wake up, lady."

She lifted her head, bleary-eyed. "What's bothering you? Can't a person get some sleep?" She put her head down again.

"Have you been tweeting?"

She sat up. "You think I'm a bird?"

"Did you see anybody else here?"

Zach whispered, "Calm, down, Chloe."

I said with a defiant note, "After the latest message from Snake Man--"

"Have you accepted Jesus Christ as your personal Lord and savior?" the woman said. "Have you been reborn of the spiritual seed?" From her backpack, she whipped out a flyer advertising a Jews for Jesus meeting.

A librarian announced over the intercom system a final call to check out books.

The woman tried to shove the flyer in my hand, but I pushed it away.

Zach slipped his arm around my shoulders. "C'mon, honey. I'll walk you to your car." He led me out of the library, to the street. "What's this about a snake man?" He slid his eyes toward mine.

"I didn't really expect him to be here." I mentioned how the cops had traced Snake Man's tweets to one of the library's computers. I told him about the Wanda's Cleaning Service imposter at Alexis' house and confessed my suspicions about him being the murderer. "I was too wired to stay away."

"What if you'd run into him? You shouldn't be taking such risks."

We crossed the street in silence. As we approached my car, the light illuminated something on the windshield. Sure enough, the city of Santa Monica had fined me forty-seven dollars for an expired meter.

I said, "Those meter maids are relentless. Where'd you park?"

"I walked over. By the time I get through the traffic, I can already be at the bookstore." He offered to follow me home after he retrieved his car.

"Not necessary. I promise to lock my doors."

The next morning, I visited Millie Gillespie, who operated out of a storefront near the Santa Monica courthouse. I took in the American flag hanging on one wall and California Bear Flag on another. She suggested we step outside, so she could have a smoke. I asked about Alexis.

"I'm pissed," Millie said, lighting up. "If the bitch doesn't show up soon, I'm hiring a bounty hunter. I intend to bring her in dead or alive."

"That's cold, Millie."

"It's a cold business." She took a puff and exhaled. "At least I won't have to feed her if she's dead."

I didn't like the way she said the word *dead*.

"Don't you have her house as collateral?"

"You think I'm in the real estate business?" She exhaled in my face.

I brought up Snake Man.

"You think I give a shit? Maybe he'll do me a favor."

We seemed to be getting nowhere fast. As she brushed an ash off her sleeve, I changed the subject to Zach.

An abstract expression crept into her eyes. "I don't know..."There's something's not quite right about that guy."

"What do you mean?"

She shrugged. "When you've worked around criminals the way I have--"

"Trust me. He's a keeper."

"Yeah?" The cigarette bobbed in her mouth.

"I checked him out thoroughly."

"You couldn't have looked too far." She dropped the butt on the sidewalk and ground it out with her foot. "Do you know he was once arrested for beating his mother?"

"Was he convicted?"

"No, but that's enough for me."

"Are you afraid of intimacy, Millie?"

"I don't see you married."

"That's because I've had so much practice, I can do for you what I can't do for myself," I stammered.

"Oh, yeah?"

Whether or not Millie was looking for the perfect man, who, in turn, was looking for the perfect woman wasn't the issue. I had to get to Alexis before she did.

I texted Marvin and requested the lowdown on Alexis' friends and acquaintances. Since I was close by, I added some quarters to my meter and trotted over to Zach's Santa Monica bookstore to let him down gently.

Zach stood on a ladder, stacking shelves in Martians, Mayhem and Magic, one of the last independent bookstores left in the city. He climbed down from his perch and threw a grin at me.

I reminded him of Sunday's Hawaiian mixer. "Will you be there?"

"Of course."

"By the way, I spoke to Millie Gillespie."

"A hopeful expression shot across his face. "What did she say?"

"To tell the truth, I've had doubts about the two of you from the start. Take my advice. Ruth's a better bet for you."

His jaw hardened. "Actually, I'd feel better if the murderer was caught first."

"How do you know it's someone in By Invitation Only?"

A man wearing a yarmulke entered the store.

Zach turned in his direction and thrust his hand in the air. "Spare me the pitch."

Zach's trade winds seemed to be blowing in the wrong direction from By Invitation Only. Never mind he promised to be at my Hawaiian mixer. Although he'd been a loyal client until now, I wondered how long he'd stick around with a murderer on the loose. Others had been slow to RSVP to the party, but they often waited until the last minute or didn't respond at all. What if I were to invite Snake Man and the cops? Yeah, right. I was trying to grow my business, not kill it.

I steered the car to Costco to pick up paper goods, drinks and hors d'oeuvres. Forget the social's Hawaiian theme. I relied on my trusty list of munchies, consisting of a large can of peanuts, bag of pretzels, assorted cheeses and box of multigrain crackers, in the event of a disappointing turnout. I stocked up on water, mai tai mix, rum and Diet Coke, but saved the pinot grigio and merlot for Trader Joe's two-buck Chuck, which was now four-buck Chuck. With the help of my Costco coupons, the bill came to sixty-eight dollars and fifty-six cents. I took out my American Express card, uncertain whether it was still good or not, and handed it to the clerk. Phew. There was a God. I proceeded to the parking lot with my purchases.

Although I survived the shopping carts and lines inside the store, I was almost killed by an overzealous driver. If I ever landed in heaven, I hoped I would never have to schlep as many bottles and packages again. I loaded up the trunk, squeezed behind the wheel and maneuvered the car to an exit.

The mid-morning traffic along Washington Boulevard barely moved. I changed lanes. A shiny black Mercedes did the same behind me. The sun's rays reflected on its windshield, masking the driver's face. I crossed the intersection, continued a couple of blocks and made a left into the alley behind my workplace. The Mercedes was still on my tail. My hands felt moist and slippery on the steering wheel. There were a lot of black Mercedes in town. What might Snake Man be driving? I tooled into my assigned space. The Mercedes parked in tandem. I glanced at my side-view mirror warily. A mop of salt-and-pepper hair preceded Marvin out of the car. He strode over to me with an unctuous air.

"Marvin, have you been following me?"

"I was in the area, looking at property."

I let myself out and leaned against my Saab. "You got my test message?"

"Hate texting."

"Thanks for sharing." I mentioned the Wanda's Cleaning Service imposter at Alexis' house.

"Not my type."

The sun accentuated the dandruff on his scalp, forehead and short-sleeve shirt.

"Who are some of Alexis' recent friends?"

"Why?"

"I have a feeling she went off with one of them."

"We don't go there."

"You're a lot of help not. Does she see any of her old buds beside you?"

"I don't think so."

"What's the story with her colleagues?"

He paused, then said in a reflective tone, "The only one I've heard her speak about is Veronica."

"Veronica?"

"Veronica Watanabe, another physicist. I understand they had a falling out--something about money." He smirked. "Isn't it always about the money?"

"I'd like to meet her."

He lowered his head. "I'm persona non grata there."

"I can't imagine why."

He said in an uppity tone, "I don't care to discuss it."

I trekked to my trunk, popped it open and reached for a couple of packages. "Make yourself useful."

He poked his nose inside a bag. "Are you having a party?"

I nodded.

"How come I wasn't invited?"

"I didn't want to spoil it."

I abandoned my previous plans to score a couple of candidates for Roger's upgraded package at the Barney's spring sale and caught the 110 to Pasadena, counting on my new BFF, the Neutronics security guard, to come through again for me. I veered past Old Town's trendy mix of revitalized living, shopping and dining, to Catalina Avenue, curious about why Marvin was in the doghouse at Neutronics R/D. I turned into the parking lot and maneuvered into a space, almost side-swiping the Buick next to me. Jeez, Louise. I sat there a moment waiting for my heart to stop thumping. Before getting out, I spruced up my hair with a pick, rolled on some raspberry lip gloss and dabbed a touch of cologne behind my ears. Ta-da. I sucked in my stomach and sashayed to the entrance.

Whoops. A different security guard was on duty at the booth. The sun felt ominous on my skin. I stepped in line behind a slight young man and a woman with fuzzy hair.

She elbowed him. "See the parrots in the trees?"

He said tongue-in-cheek, "Heard one pooped on somebody's food last week."

She giggled. "That's Pasadena for you."

The guard examined their badges and let them in. He angled his head in my direction with an unfriendly air. This could be tricky.

I inched over to him and said nonchalantly, "I'm from the Temporary Fix Agency."

He studied his clipboard. "I don't see an order here."

"I don't understand." I felt my heart race.

He stared at me. "Which department?"

I searched my purse, pretending to look for my instructions. Our gazes locked.

He said with conviction, "You're the one. You're the one who got Fred fired. I seen your picture."

Holy Bar Mitzvah.

I shook my head. "I don't know any Fred. You must have me mixed up with somebody else."

"A likely story." He threatened to call his supervisor. "Never mind, I'm going, I'm going."

I skulked to my car, wishing I had kept my plans to visit the Barney's spring sale.

"Chop, chop," the guard said behind me.

I quickened my pace.

He shouted, "This is private property, lady. Isn't it enough you got Fred fired?"

I glanced over my shoulder as the local denizen of parrots sprinkled some salt and pepper on his head.

Determined to track down Veronica Watanabe, I dialed Neutronics R/D and left a voice mail message for her. Since I was already in Pasadena, I stopped at my favorite Trader Joe's on Raymond and Fair Oaks to purchase two-buck Chuck and several bottles of champagne. In the middle of the muffin section, my Blackberry gave a shout. I tore into my purse, lifted the phone to my ear and greeted the caller.

Veronica Watanabe said in a chilly voice, "What do you want, Ms. Love?"

"How about a drink?"

"I don't drink."

"How about dinner?"

"I prefer to choose the people I eat with."

"I understand you had a falling out with Alexis Grand."

"Who told you that?"

"Marvin Smolin."

"You know Marvin?"

"He's my cousin," I said in an apologetic tone.

"Cool."

"Cool?"

"Cool."

"How about lunch?"

Twenty minutes later, I found myself sitting across the table from Veronica Watanabe, the same voluptuous brunette with the vanilla scent I'd run into previously in the Neutronics R/D elevator.

"I don't know what I was thinking," she said at the retro coffee shop on Arroyo Secco Parkway. "How I managed to mix you up with the Quick Pick lady. Mind telling me what you were doing there that day?" She speared a piece of Cobb salad with her fork.

"It's a long story."

She raised the fork to her mouth. "What's the short one?"

"Alexis wanted her patent diary."

"Why you?"

"Good question." I ran my hand along a crack in the leather seat. "Anyway, it wasn't where it was supposed to be."

Veronica chewed her food slowly. "If she'd just locked it up like everybody else…"

"How do you know she didn't?"

"Since when does Alexis Grand play by the rules?"

I nodded in acknowledgment.

"How'd you ever get in?"

"Fred."

"I don't understand where they found that security guy."

"Do you work with Alexis?"

"I don't want to talk about her. I want to talk about Marvin." She put down her fork. "What's he like?"

"Do you know him?"

"I've seen him around."

I took a sip of Diet Coke, groping for words. "He gets a little tongue-tied at times."

"Is he single?"

"He is. Would you like meet him?"

"Sure."

"I'll introduce you."

She gave me a big smile, revealing a mouthful of small teeth.

"Getting back to Alexis' patent diary, I assume the rights belong to Neutronics," I said.

"Not necessarily. We're allowed to have a few contracts of our own. I understand some lawyer was supposed to prepare a work-for-hire agreement. He didn't do it."

I almost spilled my drink. That sounded like Marvin.

"Who was the attorney?"

"Frankly, I don't give a rat's ass. I just want my seven grand back. First, Alexis hits me up for money to become a woman. The next thing I know, she's driving around in a new Porsche."

"That must have made you angry."

"You bet."

Go figure how a potential date with my cousin would produce an important lead. Alexis' research appeared to be up for grabs. She had stiffed Veronica, who seemed to have access to Alexis' patent diary and the capacity to profit from it, but did she have the intent? And where did Snake Man fit in? Too bad Veronica shut down on me before I had time pump her about the other employees.

I called Marvin and offered to introduce him to Veronica.

He said, "Somebody at Neutronics R/D thinks I'm a hottie?"

"Yes, Marvin."

"What's her net income?"

"I wouldn't know."

"How about her bra size?"

"Gross."

"What's her number?"

"Don't blow it, kid."

<hr />

After dinner, I visited the Queen Mary, not just the name of a ship but also a popular San Fernando Valley hot spot, catering to cross-dressers and transsexuals in various stages of transition and straights seeking a female-impersonation show. On the chance someone there would be able to shed some light on Alexis' whereabouts, I sprang for the twenty-dollar cover charge at the door and entered the dimly lit bar, where techno music blasted from the sound system. The room smelled like a fraternity beer bust. I surveyed the crowd, which gave new meaning to the word gender. It was clear from the frosty stares that I was an oddity. I glided over to the bar and ordered a glass of the house merlot. A candy-ass bartender uncorked a bottle of Glen Ellen. I introduced myself and said that I was a friend of Alexis Grand.

He made a sour face. "Told her not to fuck with herself. Be proud of who you are."

A man several seats away stroked his obvious black wig and said in a deep voice, "Now, don't be bitchy, Teddy. You've been acting PMSy all week."

Teddy rolled his eyes.

"Everyone acts like he's getting his period around here. I'm Sally." The man in the wig extended a beefy hand to me.

I shook it and his pinkie ring cut into my flesh. He smiled a tentative smile and I matched it. I tried to imagine how life would be with mind and body at war with one another. His over-painted face drew attention to its masculine bone structure, and his large hoop earrings added to the incongruity. He seemed to be flirting with me, but I couldn't be sure.

"How well do you know Alexis Grand?" I said within earshot of Teddy.

Teddy continued to mix drinks in silence.

Sally said, "It's a shame what happened with that janitor and all."

"When was the last time you saw her?"

"The other night. She bopped in with a guy dressed like a snake."

"Excuse me?"

"Yup, he had on a cobra mask with fangs."

"Was there a costume party going on here?"

"Not here."

"Somewhere else?"

He lifted his pair of wide-receiver shoulders to his ears.

"What was Alexis wearing?"

"Some kind of scissors getup."

"Edward Scissorhands?"

"Edward who?"

"Never mind."

"Who was the guy with her?"

"I'm terrible at names."

I took out a twenty.

"Save your money." He swiveled off the stool and clicked to the restroom on kitten heels.

I didn't catch which restroom, because the lights went out, and a spotlight shone on a man in a slinky dress, as he leaped on stage across the room.

He was no RuPaul.

I stuck around until closing time but couldn't get anybody else to talk to me beside Sally. I concluded Alexis and Snake Man had gone from Madhatter's to the Queen Mary, then to a costume party and dropped out of sight. I looked forward to catching up with Lyons and Garcia at the upcoming LAPD dinner dance and auction.

CHAPTER 15

"THE PIECES MUST FIT LIKE A SECTIONAL COUCH."

-- The Matchmaker's Bible

The LAPD annual fundraiser drew the mayor, city council and board of supervisors, as well as a sprinkling of civilians and cops to the event. I squeezed into my navy matte jersey and matching pair of three-inch heels, looped cubic zirconia drops through my ears and transferred a lipstick and handful of business cards into a silver evening bag. My bunion began to hurt. Unaccustomed to such torture, I considered changing into sensible flats, but the doorbell rang.

Sweet Pea barked.

"Daddy's here."

I hobbled downstairs with her and let Larry in.

Wagging her tail, Sweet Pea greeted him with a toy.

He threw her rubber mouse across the room and, before she could retrieve it, bent down and kissed me lightly on the lips, like old times. Don't go there, Chloe. An ex-husband isn't a real date but an illusion.

"You smell good," he said, backing away. "Don't tell me. Cashmere Mist?"

I complimented him on his sensitive nose.

"Ready to party?"

"Let's get it on."

Sweet Pea looked at us with approval in her eyes.

I leaned down and petted her head. "How do I make you understand? I know divorce is painful. Don't get your hopes up. We'll be home early."

We arrived at the Westchester Elks Club as the orchestra tuned up for the evening. Larry handed me a wheel of raffle tickets. Before I planted myself at the door, I fanned out my business cards on the reception table to entice guests who had fallen under the three-strikes law of romance.

A stream of women in party dresses and men in black tie filed into the room. Some circulated around the hors d'oeuvres table and no-host bar, whereas others socialized either in clusters, or at round tables decorated with potted topiaries and burgundy cloths. An angular sergeant from the narc division offered to purchase twenty dollars worth of raffle tickets. She inquired about my professional fee. I noticed Garcia out of the corner of my eye and excused myself from her, promising to resume our conversation later.

I caught up with Garcia at the bar, where he introduced me to his wife, whose boyish haircut complemented her delicate features and petite frame.

We exchanged pleasantries, after which I mentioned my latest communication from Snake Man.

Garcia's cell phone went off. He moved aside to take the call and then returned to us.

He said in a flat tone, "A couple of patrol officers just found a Porsche with a body in the trunk."

I started. "Alexis'?"

He hesitated. "The license plate matches."

My chest felt heavy. Had her decision to become a woman left her vulnerable in a way men weren't? Everything pointed to her being gone. I hadn't wanted to accept the possibility she was dead but had to now. There was some truth to the saying *Sometimes it's easier to appreciate a person more in death than in life.*

Garcia apologized to his wife for having to cut short their evening. From her stoic expression, she appeared to be taking it in stride.

I met his gaze. "May I come along?"

He slipped his phone in his pocket. "Don't they need you here?"

I shrugged. "You might want somebody to identify the body."

"You'd better check with your date first," he said in a lockjaw cadence, apparently unwilling to step on Larry's toes.

I located Larry backstage and gave him the facts.

"If she's dead, she's not going anywhere."

"She might be just another stiff to you but not to me."

"Can't you wait until we're done passing out the door prizes?"

As hard as it was to lose a client, it was even harder to lose one to murder--not to say anything about two. How many potential others? I left him standing there and solicited Garcia's wife, who was only too happy to draw the winning tickets from a container in exchange for a ride home.

Close to five minutes later, Garcia and I coasted out of the parking lot in his late-model Prius.

"Where's Detective Lyons?"

"That was him on the phone. He had to take his daughter to the airport. He'll be there."

I gazed at Garcia's profile, struck by the intense set of his jaw, which indicated he'd left his social side at the dance and was into his cop mode now. I asked if anyone was in custody.

Keeping his eyes on the road, he said, "A couple of kids who were caught joyriding. They're being questioned now."

"Was anybody wearing a cobra mask?"

Garcia didn't respond.

Had Alexis been carjacked? Who were these kids? Were they her type? What wasn't her type? Short pants, long pants, anything with--or without--pants. It could have been a random killing, although it was unlikely, given the recent chain of events.

I told Garcia about Alexis' date at the Queen Mary club. "Too bad Sally couldn't remember his name."

"Sally who?"

"That's not his real name."

"What is?" he said in a specious tone.

"I have no idea."

Garcia cut up Lincoln in the moonlight to the Santa Monica Freeway and sped through McClure tunnel to Pacific Coast Highway. Traffic was light at ten thirty at night. He whizzed past a sprinkling of seafood restaurants, gas stations and homes clinging to the hillside. At Topanga Canyon, he turned right, continued for about twenty minutes and made a left into a parking lot for the Will Geer outdoor Shakespeare theatre. Floodlights illuminated the area like an evening film shoot.

I got out feeling apprehensive. The crunch of gravel mixed with the sound of cricket wings. Eucalyptus permeated the night air. I struggled to maintain my balance on the uneven terrain. We signed in at a nearby table and threaded past cops milling around with coffee cups and disassociated expressions, to Lyons, who hunkered down over a red fender.

"What do we have here?" Garcia asked.

"Sorry to cut short your fun," Lyons said.

A foul stench caused me to gag. I stumbled backward wishing I had stayed behind at the dance. Lyons whipped out a jar of Vicks VapoRub from his pocket and rubbed some under my nose. Its menthol aroma counteracted the disgusting odor so that I was able to return to the Porsche. I peeked inside the trunk, where a bloated female, naked, sprawled on her side with a transparent scaly tube perched on her hip.

I glanced at Lyons. "Is that snake skin?"

Garcia looked away. "Christ."

"Get over it," Lyons snapped. "What's she doing here?"

"She's here to identify the body."

"I've got a stake in this, too."

Lyons narrowed his eyes at me. "Don't get too interested, or you might become a person of interest yourself. Now will you please step aside? You're standing on evidence."

I backed away.

Garcia wiped his face with a handkerchief. "Did someone call a herpetologist?"

Lyons shouted, "Very good. Your education is showing." He turned to me with a quizzical look. "Is that your client, Alexis Grand, Ms. Love?"

I nodded, observing the bruises on her neck. Was I next? I shivered, giving serious thought to joining the NRA.

Lyons inquired about Alexis' next of kin. I mentioned her son.

I stared at the corpse, transfixed. "I didn't realize Porsche trunks were big enough for six footers."

Lyons shrugged. "Somebody must have dumped her there before rigor mortis set in."

"Was there anything else beside a body in there?"

He said with a sarcastic note, "It would certainly be a tight fit."

A uniformed cop with pale eyebrows and lashes handed Lyons a corn dog. My glance hung on the fast food while he bit into it. Apparently, people could get used to anything.

"What's the deal with the scissors on her wrists?" the cop with pale eyebrows and lashes asked.

"Can't you see? It's part of a costume," Lyons said.

"Edward Scissorhands," I added.

"Imagine her trying to shave with those things," Lyons' lips parted in a greasy smile. He took another bite of corn dog.

I laughed from the same nervousness that makes a person whistle in a graveyard.

Garcia continued to keep his distance. "What about the kids in custody?"

"They don't appear to know anything."

Lyons shoved the last bit of corn dog into his mouth and rubbed his hands together. "Notice the bruises on her legs. Do you think she was raped?" he said to no one in particular.

Millie Gillespie elbowed her way in like a drill sergeant. "Hey, guys, heard the news on my scanner. I was sure I was going to have to eat this one. "Guess I won't now." She smiled brightly. "You'll get me a copy of the death certificate, yes?"

"We always do, Millie. Now go home and be a good girl," Lyons said.

She lifted Garcia's hand and scrutinized the handkerchief. "Is that one of mine?"

Garcia examined the linen square. "Now that you mention it..."

"It's for dress, not for blowsy." She tweaked his nose.

⋙⋰ ⋱⋘

The sun was coming up by the time we left the Will Geer parking lot. I kicked off my shoes and made some notes on my BlackBerry. Things to investigate: Who had the motivation, capacity and access to kill Alexis? To-do list: Locate the Wanda's Cleaning Service impersonator. Find out more about Alexis' colleagues at Neutronics R/D. Get hold of the autopsy reports for both Alexis and Fong. Talk to Marvin about the seventeen, five Alexis still owed me.

My thoughts segued to Sweet Pea. I glanced at my watch. Never mind dogs have no sense of time. This was the first night I had ever left mine alone. My stomach lurched. Had I turned off the oven?

A half hour later, I raced up the walkway to my townhouse with my keys out and shoes in hand. The spring perfume gave no indication of a fire inside the house. I heard Sweet Pea's bark and smiled. We were going to have nice dreams, dreams of princes and princesses, debutantes and cadets, showgirls and producers.

Then I thrust open the door. No more dreams of princes and princesses. Dreams of apples with worms.

CHAPTER 16

"A MATCHMAKER MUSTN'T BE SHY."

Something blocked the entrance to my townhouse, blonde and hairy, like Alexis dog. Holy crap. It *was* Alexis' dog. Puppy lay there lifeless with his eyes open. A fetid odor emanated from his swollen body and I retched. Who had done this? Too bad dogs can't talk. Sweet Pea barked and yelped. I climbed over the carcass, cast aside my purse and scooped up Sweet Pea. She wrapped her paws around my neck and clung to me like a necklace. I stroked her body, trying to soothe her. If the bastard thought he could stop me, he was loco. Was he still here? I flipped open the Swiss Army knife attached to my key ring. Never mind the blade was less than two inches long. It was still capable of stabbing somebody and drawing blood. I maneuvered Sweet Pea to my shoulder and traversed the living and dining rooms with her.

"Come out, come out, wherever you are," I shouted.

I waited a moment.

No response.

I continued to the kitchen.

Silence.

I proceeded to the powder room and upstairs, into the master suite with my heart pounding. Was he playing with me? I planted my feet in anticipation. He appeared to be gone. I retreated to my car with Sweet Pea, leaving behind a pool of vomit and decomposing dog.

An ambulance screamed down Walgrove Avenue. I slammed on the brakes envisioning myself inside with an eight-foot boa for a necklace. Who would attend me? Did ERs have access to veterinarians? How much would my insurance pay for triage? I began to cry. As soon as the ambulance passed by, I stepped on the accelerator. I tore past Venice Boulevard to Larry's Mar Vista bungalow.

When I arrived, I found Larry in the middle of watering his plants on his porch. I shot into his driveway and set the brake. He acknowledged me in stony silence.

I rushed across his lawn, barefoot and sobbing. "Somebody killed Alexis Grand's dog. They broke into my house and left him for me."

He bent down and flicked a snail off a pot of dill. "If you want sympathy, you've come to the wrong place. This isn't my case, you know."

I wiped away the tears with the back of my hand. "Don't tell me you're still carrying a grudge from last night. You are, aren't you?" The scent of morning dew filled my nostrils.

"You don't owe me anything. We're not married anymore."

"Martyr."

A plumbing truck whizzed past us.

Larry straightened up and trained his eyes on Sweet Pea. She stood on her hind legs sniffing his Roma tomatoes. Before she had time to dig in, he yanked her away.

"Did you speak to Lyons and Garcia?"

I shook my head. "Not yet."

He said in a detached tone, "What are you waiting for?"

"How can you be so callous?" I heard my voice crescendo.

"Control yourself. You'll wake the neighbors." He offered me his iPhone.

As soon as I changed my locks, I wasn't about to give Mr. Curmudgeon a key.

"Mind if I leave Sweet Pea here?"

"Just don't make it too long."

I tore over to my townhouse to meet Lyons and Garcia, pulled up next to a squad car at the curb and rolled down my window.

An unfamiliar cop was behind the wheel.

I introduced myself.

"What's this about a dog?" he said.

The sun angled across his face, partially hiding his features, unlike the chevron and hash marks on his sleeve. I briefed him about Puppy.

His partner thumbed through a reg book. "It says here animals aren't considered murder. They're malicious destruction of property, which is only a misdemeanor."

"Not a felony?"

The cop behind the wheel climbed out of the car. His badge said **OFFICER MARCOS**. Somewhere in his forties, he had a schnoz that stretched across his face like a rubber band.

"We understand your frustration, lady. Officer Utley and I both have dogs. If you want a nice neat life, go to Merced. Nothing ever happens there beside some farmer getting drunk."

His partner stepped out on the passenger side, revealing a mottled café-au-lait complexion.

"Are Lyons and Garcia on their way?"

"Dogs are our jurisdiction," Marcos said.

"What about snakes?"

"No snakes," he said nonchalantly.

I parked and led them into the house. The sickening odor of death and puke accosted my nose and I almost lost my cookies again. I rushed inside and pushed back the sliding glass door to let in some fresh air. Utley broke out the Vicks, an apparent department staple, which he passed to me. The menthol aroma succeeded at calming my stomach. He snatched his cell phone from a pocket and summoned Animal Services to pick up the dead dog.

"Is somebody going to do an autopsy?" I returned the jar to Utley.

His partner said with a condescending air, "The department doesn't employ medical examiners for animals."

I offered to call my vet.

"Isn't that against the rules?" Utley sounded as if he were going for extra credit.

"You think?"

Marcos took a statement from me on his iPad. I tagged along while he and Utley combed the house for clues. They concluded there was no evidence of forced entry.

"Who has access to your house?" Marcos asked.

"Nobody who had a connection to the dog or its owner." I paused. "The person sounds like the one who put the snake in my office. Did you read the report?"

"No time for that." Marcos chewed his lip, calling attention to his pronounced schnoz. "We came as soon as we got the call."

"If you had, you'd know about Snake Man."

"Pardon me?"

I repeated the story, which he noted on his iPad.

"Did your neighbors see anyone?"

"I suggest you check with them."

Marcos directed Utley to check the premises for a witness.

The same Animal Services officer from before showed up later with another burlap sack but no gummy bears this time. She slipped on a mask and pair of surgical gloves, leaned over the lifeless dog and ran her fingers over his frame.

She looked back at Marcos. "Remember a couple of years ago when that six-foot boa did a job on that studio animal trainer in Burbank?"

"She's pretty good at this," Marcos said to me with a mirthful note.

I countered, "How do you know he wasn't run over by a car or poisoned?"

"The skeleton feels more like he was squeezed," the Animal Services officer said in a confident voice.

She could have fooled me. While she finished with Puppy, I called a locksmith to change my tumblers.

By the time the locksmith arrived, the dog had been removed from the living room, the floor cleaned up and the smell of vomit and death gone.

"Chloe Love," he said with a perplexed expression. "How do I know the name?"

"I'm a matchmaker."

"The one on the news..." He rested his tool chest on the ground and tapped his head. "Duh. Do you have any clients left?" His breath smelled like coffee.

I snapped at him. "Don't you think I'm still in business?"

"I didn't mean no harm." The innocent look in his eye appeared to confirm it. "I'd sure like to find a nice lady. Do you have any other transsexuals?"

I stared at him. "Sorry, you're out of luck."

New locks or not, I didn't feel safe in my house. I contemplated replacing my bogus ADT sign with an armed response system, complete with surveillance cameras and medical alert button. But medical alert buttons were for the elderly who fell in closets and needed CPR. I wasn't there yet. And forget about the cost of one. Whoever broke in ought to be capable of tripping an alarm. Someone had strangled Fong and left a boa at the scene. He had killed Alexis and her dog and wasn't about to leave me out of the loop.

I climbed into bed for the night with Sweet Pea. What had set off the killing spree? Why was Alexis' patent diary missing? Who were some of the obvious people to benefit?

Juanita Arroyo topped my list. Never mind she was female, She'd have no trouble ordering the death of an errant husband or his lover. The Wanda's Cleaning Service imposter couldn't be ruled out, either. What about Marvin? On second thought, Mr. Fifteen Percent was too much of a wuss to murder anything bigger than a hamster. Veronica Watanabe struck me as another possibility. The same was true for Alexis' other coworkers and her ex-wife, whom I'd yet to meet. Then there was Polly. She'd like nothing better than to put me out of business, although she was more inclined to resort to rumors and client theft than murder. What about Zach? He had no connection to either Fong or Alexis.

Besides, why rescue me from a boa if he intended to kill me? He was more interested in getting in my pants.

I dozed intermittently until my alarm went off in the morning. I eyed the clock on my nightstand. Six thirty. Time to rise, if not shine. I hoisted myself out of bed. Sweet Pea beat me to the carpet. I shimmied into a warm-up suit, grabbed my keys and her leash.

The early morning air felt mild. I voted for a mild day. I stopped at my mailbox, unlocked it and pulled out the latest edition of *Pet Edge* magazine. The cover featured a Maltese with a toy rubber magenta sandal in its mouth. Sweet Pea would love another chewie. Too bad I couldn't afford the ninety-nine cents. I reached inside for the rest of my mail. Along with a Bloomie's catalogue and introductory offer to *Cooking Light*, there was a letter from the IRS. I hadn't spoken to Hank in a while. I opened the envelope and learned the IRS intended to attach my bank account, unless I came up with seventeen, five by the end of the month. So much for a mild day.

I dashed inside, and texted Hank, demanding to know what happened to the IRS' consumer-friendliness programs.

All bets are off.

I didn't know any were on.

Because of you, my Edsel blew up.

I tried to warn you.

My Edsel, my beautiful Edsel.

With barely enough money to pay the rent, let alone the IRS, I gave Marvin a jingle. Thanks to his secretary, I located him on the tennis court at Rancho Park, which was easy to find because of its fen shui to Century City and Beverly Hills. Coincidentally, it backed up to my favorite eighteen-hole public golf course. Never mind my set of clubs was in the trunk of my car. I could resist temptation.

I eased out of the car, scoped the landscape and set my alarm. As I jogged past a group of octogenarians of mixed persuasions, some amazingly agile while they engaged in Tai Chi, the grass felt damp against my legs. I nearly tripped over a man, interfering with his crouching tiger pose. When I recovered, I threaded past the pool area to the courts, where a series of hollow pops hung in the air.

Marvin was in the middle of a volley, so I waited for him to finish his point before I called out to him.

He jerked around and shielded his eyes from the sun with his hand. "How'd you find me here?"

"I spoke to your secretary."

He said under his breath, "She shouldn't be telling people where I am. I'll have to talk to her."

I asked if he had been in touch with Veronica Watanabe.

He said with a smug expression, "We have a date this weekend."

"That's wonderful, Marvin. You'll have to let me know how it goes."

I unlocked the gate and joined him on the tennis court. He introduced me to his opponent, who displayed a ready smile. Had the man's wedding band not gleamed in the morning sunshine, I would have offered him a By Invitation Only free trial membership. I shoved the IRS letter in Marvin's hand. He didn't have his reading glasses with him, so I paraphrased the contents for him.

"You're lucky the market's been good to me lately, and if it's good to me, it's going to be good for my loved ones. Just give me a chance to get to the office."

Had I caught Mr. Fifteen Percent in a weak moment? Was it because of the presence of his tennis partner, his introduction to Veronica Watanabe or a guilty conscience? I wasn't about to question the reason and thanked him for his generosity.

Before I collected my check from Marvin, I hauled myself into By Invitation Only to receive a delivery of tables and chairs for my Hawaiian mixer. Juanita loped into my lobby, flanked by a pair of steroid cases.

She stood across from me, tapping her foot. "Where the hell's Alexis Grand?"

"Don't you know she's dead?"

Juanita stopped tapping. "You're lying."

"Do I look like I'm lying?"

One of the steroid cases lit a stinky cigar and blew smoke in my face.

"Where's her bomb manual?" Juanita said.

"Beats me," I croaked.

I remembered an old ashtray in the back of my drawer and started over to it.

"Don't fuck with us, bitch," the bruiser with stringy hair said. He reached for my ear and twisted it until I heard a high-pitched hum.

"I'm a matchmaker, match-maker, marriage broker." To keep from fainting, I said, "There's a drawing for a trip to Hawaii tomorrow night. If you'd like to drop your business cards in the slot..." Juanita's flat gaze met mine. "No business cards."

The bruiser with stringy hair let go of my ear. I reached for it amazed it was still there.

"We'll be in touch again," Juanita said.

I rubbed my lobe trying to feel it. If Juanita didn't know Alexis was dead, she couldn't have killed her. That was a no-brainer. She could have been lying, but I didn't think so. With her no longer a member of my inner circle of suspects, the Wanda's Cleaning Service imposter hurtled to front-row center.

CHAPTER 17

"ONE OF THESE DAYS IS LIKE NONE OF THESE DAYS."

--- *The Matchmaker's Bible*

I showed up at Marvin's office, still favoring my ear. The receptionist appraised me with bulging eyes. "Your ear--it's swollen."

I took my hand away. "Yes, I know."

A woman with duckbill lips glided over to the receptionist.

"I'm Jill Grand, Marvin's eleven o'clock," she said in a halting cadence.

"Grand as in Alexis?" I stared at her enhanced lips.

She was about the same size as Alexis but looked as if she had been born and raised in the female gender.

"I think I knew your husband."

"You mean my ex?" Jill was careful to correct me.

Marvin loomed in the doorway, smelling as if he'd poured a bottle of Old Spice cologne on himself. He started to introduce us, but Jill intervened.

"We've already met."

A tense silence followed.

"I thought we were happy." She lifted her shoulders to her ears. "What do you say to your husband when he comes home from work one day and whispers in your ear that he's a woman?" She grimaced. "What do you tell your kids?"

Marvin wandered over to me with interest. "Your ear--it's all red and puffy."

"Yes, I know."

He zeroed in on me like a vulture. "What happened?"

I stepped away from him. "Don't touch."

Jill cut in. "What's the story with my spousal support?"

Marvin urged her to follow him inside. "Don't worry your pretty little head."

"Screw you, Marvin. Is there a will?"

She appeared to know her customer.

"Yes, there's a will, and the court will appoint some-one to handle the estate, until Ethan is--"

"Appoint someone? What about his own mother?"

"What do you want from me? It was Alexis' choice."

"I'm going to fight this," she said with a menacing expression.

"Be my guest."

She marched to the door and shut it behind her.

He muttered, "She works for the Audubon Society tracking bird migration patterns."

"No blue jays for her. More like crows."

"She thought she'd be set."

"What about me?"

He cast his arm around my shoulder. "I was just get-ting to you, my dear cousin. With Bakersfield the fastest growing city in the country, we can open a By Invitation Only satellite office, complete with personal life coach and concierge service." A crafty smile spread across his lips. "What do you say about becoming partners?"

I wiped the dandruff off his jacket. "Now you ex-pect fifty percent?"

"How about twenty-five?"

"Pass."

Forget Marvin. I continued to worry about how I was going to come up with the rest of the dough for the IRS. Four new clients at five thou a pop ought to be enough to put me in the black. No more fooling around. On second thought, if the murderer showed up at my Hawaiian mixer, it might be a moot point.

I returned to my office. Pulling out all stops, I left a last-minute come-one, come-all message on Facebook, Twitter and my By Invitation Only website and turned off my laptop.

Marvin trundled in and pressed something in my hand.

"What's this?"

"My check--You forgot my check."

I glanced down and realized he had given me a postdated one. "I have to square myself with God and my country now,"

"Picky, picky."

I started to return it to him, but he removed his fingers from mine.

"Keep it. You might need it."

I thanked him begrudgingly.

By five p.m. the next evening, I'd finished decorating the courtyard with fisherman's nets, shells and tiki gods. I'd put out refreshments and was ready to greet my guests. Decked out in a floral sundress and plastic orchid behind my ear, I passed out leis to the catchy beat of a Hawaiian war chant.

Zach moseyed in, sporting an islands shirt over jeans.

He gazed at the turn out with uncertainty. "Where's Millie?"

"She's not coming."

His face reflected disappointment.

"I'm afraid she's not serious about meeting anybody."

"Neither am I now. I'm just here to support you."

I smiled with appreciation. Taking his hand, I said, "You might as well make the most of the night. Let me introduce you to some lovely ladies."

He withdrew his fingers. "You're the best-looking--"

Just then, Juanita Arroyo burst in, resembling an extreme-makeover graduate. My right eye developed a tick. Terrorists didn't take Hawaiian vacations. They took terrorists vacations. I excused myself from Zach.

Anxious to get rid of Juanita without an embarrassing scene, I speeded up the drawing for the free trip to Hawaii. I stopped the music, faked a drum roll and reached into the entry box next to my guest book.

I paused. "The winner of the Maui vacation for two is…the winner is…Juanita Arroyo.

She cackled and jumped up and down.

I grabbed my camera.

She charged toward me and knocked the Canon out of my hand. "No pictures."

Zach said with a puzzled expression. "Who's that?"

I picked up the punch bowl. "International business, geographically undesirable."

Early the following day, I visited the IRS drop-in center to work out a payment plan with the government. Most of the citizens filling out official forms downtown appeared to be Spanish speakers. If I didn't know better, I would think Hispanics were the only ones who paid their taxes. I proceeded to the information booth and showed the receptionist my letter.

As she lowered her head to read, her auburn bob fell into her eyes. She pushed the strands behind her ears, only to have them land on her face again. She lifted her chin and directed me to a payment box on the wall.

I paused. "Actually, I don't have all the money yet."

She said matter-of-factly, "We have problem-solving days on Tuesdays."

"I could be dead by Tuesday."

She blinked. "We're not equipped to take appointments here. You'll have to contact the Fresno office, which you can find listed on our website."

The letter said that I had thirty days to pay up. I opened my wallet and found Marvin's postdated check. At least I was responding in a timely manner. Let them chase me for the interest and penalties.

I celebrated the end of the IRS chapter with a cup of Starbucks from across the street. A woman at the next table wearing an Angry Birds T-shirt conjured up the image of Jill Grand. Her lips superimposed over my cup. She had pitched quite a fit in Marvin's office. That was an understatement. I took a sip of decaf, which scalded my tongue, and put down the cup. Could Jill's anger toward her ex-husband have driven her over the edge with him? I reached for my cell phone and dialed information to see if she were listed. No Jill Grand. The closest I came was to a J. Grand in Encino. I had no idea where she lived but asked the operator to connect me. A voice on the answering machine sounded like hers, although I couldn't be sure. I finished my decaf quickly and traipsed to my car filled with a certain fascination for the person who had married Alex aka Alexis. I popped open the trunk and removed a By Invitation Only brochure, intending to drop it off at Jill's house and follow up in a couple of days.

The mid-afternoon sun felt healing. Would that it could prevent violence. What a concept! I maneuvered into traffic and shot up the Hollywood Freeway to the San Fernando Valley, which was invariably ten degrees warmer than downtown L.A. I flipped down my visor. Even through the windows, the sun seared my skin like a branding iron. I got off at Havenhurst, crossed

Ventura and continued south of the boulevard, the way locals referred to as the right side of the tracks. In my book, both sides of Ventura Boulevard represented miles of heat, leading to more miles and miles of the same. Jacarandas shrouded the residential streets in a purple canopy.

I located the address in my purse, passed a run-down Cape Cod in the middle of the block and slowed down. Bingo. The numbers on the house matched it. I pulled into the driveway, climbed out of the car and scooted past a dead lawn to the front door. Never mind ringing the bell. I slid the By Invitation Only brochure through the mail slot as bird song spilled from the windows. The door swung open and a boy leaned against the jam. He couldn't be more than fourteen. He had Alexis' pronounced jaw and brown hair but blue eyes. I saw something wrapped around his arm that glinted like a piece of jewelry. Then it reared its head.

CHAPTER 18

"MARRIAGES ARE MADE IN MATCHMAKER HEAVEN."

-- *The Matchmaker's Bible*

The boy invited me in, kicked the door shut behind us and gestured to the snake.

"Wanna feel?" His voice broke and changed pitch.

I backed away. "No, thanks."

He chuckled. "They're attracted to heat, you know, and they like to congregate around your pulse spots."

He seemed to enjoy the attention as much as Alexis had relished the spotlight. The sunlight accentuated the peach fuzz above his lip and on his cheeks.

"How long do you think it takes for a ferret to poop?".

"You're into ferrets, too?"

The conversation began to sound like a harbinger of more unpleasant things to come.

"A ferret takes an hour, but a shrew poops constantly. Do you know how long it takes for a boa?" he asked.

"Frankly, I've never thought about it, but it's an interesting question. Where do you go to school?"

"Milliken."

"The middle school?"

He nodded.

Gazing at the white chain-link pattern across the boa's brown body, I said, "I'm looking for a snake like yours."

His glance wandered to my feet. "Why? Are you gonna kill it? Any person with leather shoes on..."

I shook my head. "Road kill."

He gave me a skeptical look. "There's this website called Medusa.com."

"Like the woman with the snakes in her hair?"

He smiled, as if I'd won a couple of points from him. "My mom gave me Pretzel for my birthday."

I handed him one of my business cards.

He inclined his head to the side. Hey, aren't you the matchmaker my dad signed up with?"

"Uh-huh."

"Thought so."

"You must be Ethan Grand. I'm so sorry about your father. When was the last time you saw him?"

He shrugged. "Not for a long time." He took a step toward me. So what happened to him?"

"I'm trying to find out."

He said with a tentative expression, "Do I look like him?"

I nodded. "You're intelligent like him, too."

"That's all we have in common," he said with the forced machismo of an adolescent struggling to find his own sexual identity.

I heard a motorcycle and turned to the window, as it rumbled to a stop in the driveway. Pregnant lips jumped off, followed by the driver. I followed Ethan outside. He loped over to her, giggling, and shoved the boa under her nose.

She backed away. "Watch yourself, kid, or I'm getting rid of Pretzel."

Her biker sweetie looked fleetingly in my direction, hopped back on his Harley and roared off.

"That was quick," I said, sensing my presence had set off something in him.

Jill acknowledged me on the sidewalk with a pout. "Do you know Tony?"

"Should I?"

Suspicion glinted in her eyes. "He seemed to know you."

"Tony who?"

Ethan said with contempt, "Tony Hammond."

"The name doesn't sound familiar."

"My boyfriend gets around." She pursed her over-sized lips. "What are you doing here, anyway?"

Ethan said, "She dropped something off for you."

I shrugged. "I thought you might need my services. Now that I'm here, maybe not."

Did Tony and I know each other? Who could tell with a pair of goggles and helmet hiding his mug? What did Jill mean by her boyfriend getting around?

I stopped at a gas station, filled up the tank and returned to the office, where I consulted my By Invitation Only rejects file. Tony Hammond wasn't among the applicants. I sat down at the computer and Googled the name. I found a rear admiral, Anthony Hammond, who had died in 2000, an Anthony Charles Hammond who was the current musical director of the London symphony and Anthony P, Hammond, a classics professor who had operated a successful loan business on the side, until he was nailed for defrauding his UC Santa Barbara colleagues out of their homes and given a scholarship to the Lompoc federal pen. I swiveled back and forth in my leather chair, causing it to squeak. Who had I run into lately with a PhD in classics? The Wanda's Cleaning Service imposter. Holy smokes. No wonder he'd been quick to take a powder when he saw me. What in the hell was Jill doing with another guy in women's clothing? Go figure what floats a person's boat.

The sound of my landline startled me. I yanked the receiver from its cradle and answered.

Madeleine said between sobs, "Brian isn't talking to me."

"What happened?"

"He accused my son of drawing blood."

"Your son bit Brian?"

"Jason didn't mean any harm."

"If your objective is marriage, Madeleine, you'd better muzzle your kid."

"But--"

"No buts." I hurried her off the phone.

Anxious to resume my research, I located the Medusa website, clicked on it and browsed through the merchandise. A window popped open advertising *Exotic Animals*. It seemed to be an online version of the catalogue I'd found in Alexis' desk. It listed a toll-free number and Iowa post office box. I grabbed my BlackBerry, punched in the ten digits and bypassed the automated message to reach a company representative. I heard a familiar Midwestern twang on the other end.

"This is Alexis Grand," I fibbed. "We spoke earlier about my boa that arrived dead--in L.A."

"I remember you."

"So, I've been rethinking my order and wonder if it could be under Jill Grand."

"Thought you said your name was Alexis."

"Alexis Jill."

Silence.

"Date of purchase?"

"Some time before March fifth--I can't tell you the exact..."

"Credit card?"

"Pardon my senior moment."

"We have our privacy rules. I can't just go looking up things without an order number, credit card or date."

"Just a minute. How about the shipping address?"

"What is it?" she said reluctantly.

I scrambled for Jill Grand's and supplied it to her.

The rep consulted her computer. "Says here we sent a boa there on March ninth." She paused. "Looks like it's still under warranty. How about an anaconda this time?"

"After the last one died--"

"That wasn't an anaconda."

"Just the same."

I plunked down the phone, realizing March ninth was too late for the snake coiled around Fong's body and the one in my office but not for Jill's gift to her son, Ethan. Still, it didn't account for the two boas in question or how the *Exotic Animals* catalogue had landed in Alexis's drawer. I checked my watch. Robert were about to tie the knot that evening. Although I had more work to do, I shut down my computer, unwilling to miss this golden moment.

After a mani/pedi at the local nail joint, I slipped into a lavender silk dress and pair of silver ankle straps and did the makeup thing with an eye for the camera. I loved weddings, as long as they weren't mine. I tossed a pashmina over my shoulders and tucked a lipstick into a beaded clutch bag. Equipped with my Canon, I set out for the shindig, looking forward to photographing By Invitation Only's first marriage. What better advertisement for a matchmaker than a wedding?

I cut over to the city of Santa Monica. The sunset looked as vibrant as the inside of a blood orange. I spun over to the Fairmont Hotel, which overlooked the Pacific Ocean and Palisades Park. A sea of twinkle lights dotted the front entrance. I pulled up to the valet, turned over my car to him and snapped a picture of the festive exterior before disappearing into the five-diamond venue.

The leaf-print carpet represented commercialism in its lowest form, in contrast to the rest of the

appointments. The interior designer must've been related to the general manager or have gotten a special
deal. I veered past a potted palm, heard my name above
the rumble of voices and turned in the direction.

Robert confronted me, shaking. "The wedding's
off."

I grabbed his tuxedo and pinned him against a
marble pillar. "What is this shit?"

He looked away. "I just haven't figured out what to
say to the guests."

"Where's Patricia?"

"Late. Late for the pictures. Late, late, late. Do you
think I want to spend the next fifty years with somebody who's always late? I don't think so."

I gazed at the guests streaming into the Royal
Dalton room. "What about *your* flaws, like impatience?
Come on, sport. Don't give up on her. Trust me. I've
been through this hundreds of times before."

He stared at me with an oblique expression.

"Don't do this to me. Can't you pretend? If it
doesn't work out, I'll help you get an annulment. At
fifty-nine, you're not just having cold feet, they're frost-
bitten. Shape up, Robert. Cut the crap." I cuffed his
chin. "Buck up."

Silence.

He turned toward the room tentatively.

"Go on." I gave him a shove. "I'll be waiting for
you." I made a beeline for the door.

The Homeland Security hunk strode over to me and twitched a smile.

Taken aback, I asked, "Do you know Robert and Patricia?"

He shook his head. "We found your business card with a couple of plane tickets on Juanita Arroyo this morning."

CHAPTER 19
"EVERY PATH HAS A PUDDLE."
-- *The Matchmaker's Bible*

The cut of the hunk's navy blue suit accentuated his broad shoulders and trim waistline.

I took hold of his arm and walked him into the lobby. "How did you find me here?"

"It was no secret."

"I see you've been checking my website."

He stopped in front of a still life of a ham sandwich, some walnuts and glass of milk.

I whispered, "This isn't good for my business. Can't it wait?"

He gave me the evil eye. "How well do you know Juanita Arroyo?"

I let go of his arm. "Enough to be convinced I want nothing to do with her."

"Why'd you spring for a trip to Hawaii?"

So that was it. Focusing on the ham sandwich in the painting, I said, "I was trying to get rid of her. It seemed like the expedient thing to do."

"Why didn't you call us?"

I said dryly, "With your McCarthy tactics?"

His lips pulled back in a taut smile.

"It was part of a promotion. She found out about the contest."

"She claims she never entered a contest."

I hesitated. "What else did the bitch say?"

"Are you working for her?"

I blinked. "I already told you her husband was working for me as my janitor."

"We understand you made a large cash deposit recently."

"I deposited it to pay the IRS. Can I help it if one of my clients doesn't believe in paying by check or credit card? Talk to Cousin Marvin about Alexis Grand. It's all his fault anyway."

By the time the hunk finished with me, the ceremony was over. I crept into the reception hall in time to join the receiving line. I hoped Patricia and Robert hadn't noticed my absence. They appeared to be past their nervousness and all lovey-dovey again. I queued up with the other guests to congratulate the happy couple. When it was my turn, Patricia and Robert insisted on posing with me for a photo. I seized the opportunity to shoot some pictures of my own.

During cocktail hour, I ran into Zach, attired in a T-shirt and jeans--hardly the makings of black-tie optional.

"What are you doing here, Zach?"

"My uncle's staying at the hotel. I recognized Patricia's name on the door and figured you might be here." He gave me the once-over. "Hey, I like your dress." He paused. "I really like your dress." He lifted an eyebrow. "The whole package isn't bad either."

Flattery was a powerful aphrodisiac.

I shoved my champagne flute in his hand. "When am I going to get you married off?"

"Maybe one of these days I'll be able to break you down."

"Don't hold your breath."

"What if I were to drop out of By Invitation Only?"

I tugged on his sleeve. "Please don't do me any favors."

"How else am I going to improve my chances with you?"

"You need to be more open-minded."

He stole a shrimp off my hors d'oeuvres plate. "Says who?"

"Says me."

The doors parted for dinner and Zach made a quick exit. I continued to the dining room and checked my reflection in the mirror. I smoothed my skirt with my hands. Maybe I wasn't as invisible as I thought.

The wedding ended close to eleven. I entered the parking lot, looking forward to sorting through my photos of the event. I handed my claim ticket to the valet and waited for my car under an awning.

A pregnant woman next to me said," Aren't you the matchmaker who introduced Robert to Patricia?"

The man with her laughed. "She either gets them married, or murdered."

I shoved my face in his. "Listen, buster, my track record isn't bad. This is my fifteenth wedding."

Okay, so I was exaggerating a bit.

"Don't mind my husband." The woman elbowed him. "Shut up, Stanley."

Stanley smelled as if he had knocked back one too many champagnes. The valet delivered my Saab and I burned rubber getting out of there. I made a right on Second Street and heard a scratching sound that appeared to be coming from my glove compartment. I passed Wilshire Boulevard. The noise intensified. I stopped at the curb, turned off the motor and listened. The annoyance persisted. I popped open my glove compartment. Something sprang out, tongue flashing.

I jumped out of the car, trembling. This wasn't the kind of wedding favor I anticipated. Oy, Gutanyu. Had Tony Hammond been at the hotel? Could somebody else beside him have put the snake there? I sprinted back to the Fairmont parking lot, passing tourists, moviegoers and locals in the damp night air. The valet shot a surprised look at me.

"How the hell did a snake get in my car?" I shouted.

The valet threw up his hands.

Another parking attendant approached me with an authoritative air. "What's the problem, lady?"

I repeated my story. His Majesty took out a note pad and wrote down: *One snake in glove compartment.*

"How many snakes do you get?"

He deliberated a moment. "We had a gerbil once and a chicken." He identified himself as the supervisor and spoke to the valet in what sounded like Russian.

"Well?"

The supervisor put away his pad of paper. "He appreciates your tip."

"That's all?"

"And he doesn't know anything about the snake."

I handed him a five.

He said dismissively, "It was a short fat man with a moustache."

"Not a biker or some guy in drag?"

The supervisor shepherded me over to a parking attendant's booth and showed me a sign in the window, which stated the management wasn't responsible for theft or damage to vehicles.

I called the cops.

By the time Lyons met me at my car, the snake had slithered away. Lyons checked under the seats, in the gutter and on the sidewalk with his flashlight.

He said in a pissed tone, "You call this evidence?"

I shrugged. "It got away."

"I'll bet."

"Are you doubting me?" I waved my clutch bag in his face, put off by his condescending attitude. "It was red, black and yellow, you know, friend of fellow."

"Don't tell me you were a Girl Scout."

I held up two fingers. "Red, yellow and black, watch out Jack."

He produced a bottle of prescription pills and popped one in his mouth. Although I couldn't read the label, I had a feeling it might be Xanax. He swallowed it without water.

His brow furrowed. "The snake must have been awfully small to fit into a glove compartment."

"What difference does it make?"

"Any idea who put it there?"

As I mentioned Tony Hammond, my Blackberry sang out. I was tempted to let it ring but lacked the necessary willpower. I poked in my purse for my phone. A blocked number showed up on its display panel. I pushed the talk button.

"I know who this is," I said, losing it."

Marvin replied, "What the hell did you get me into?"

My life felt suddenly like a Fellini movie.

"Did you put a snake in my glove compartment?"

"What's the matter with you? Have you flipped out on me? By the way, how'd you come up with that grand-prize winner of yours?"

It took me a moment to realize Marvin was talking about Juanita Arroyo. "It's a long story. The short one is I was trying to get her off my back."

"So now Homeland Security's on mine. Thank you very much. They think we've been laundering money."

"You know that's not true."

He hesitated. "But they don't and I don't need the Feds in my business."

"What are you up to now, Marvin?"

He cleared his throat. "Those guys know how to find dirty laundry even with the pope.

≈⊱ ⊰≈

I could hardly bring myself to get into the car the next morning. The idea of a snake making itself comfortable inside my glove compartment gave me a case of the willies. What if the thing wasn't gone? Let somebody else be the one to find it. I hustled to the nearest car wash and splurged on a detail job. Fortunately, my American Express card which I'd been saving for an emergency was still good. While I waited in a lawn chair, I took out my cell phone and called Marvin. In all the excitement of the night before, I'd forgotten to ask him about his date with Veronica.

"How'd it go?" I said with trepidation.

"We really hit it off."

"I hope you behaved yourself, Marvin."

"You would have been proud of me. I was the quintessential gentleman. Have you spoken to Veronica?"

I hung up from him, got in touch with her immediately and said, "I understand you had a good time with my cousin. So, was it a successful match?"

She slammed down the phone.

Was Marvin hallucinating? He never failed to disappoint. Too bad Veronica closed the door on me before I could finagle another invitation to Neutronics R/D and get to know some of Alexis' other colleagues. I picked up the local *Argonaut* newspaper and skimmed through it aimlessly. The calendar section advertised a reunion of Bronx high school graduates who had relocated to the west coast. I'd grown up in L.A., but Larry hailed from the Bronx. I sent him a text message to inform him about the gathering and learned he was home with the flu. He was hardly ever sick until he became a vegetarian.

An hour later, I showed up on his doorstep armed with a can of mock chicken soup and his favorite dog. He greeted us in his pajamas, looking wan and gray.

"Enter at your own risk," he said in a hoarse voice.

I kept my distance from him and threaded past his chocolate- brown leather recliner beside a sixty-inch TV, on which he was given to watching his collection of *Hawaii Five-O*, *Dragnet* and *Adam-12* DVDs. Sweet Pea scurried past us, taking inventory of changes since her last visit.

The house smelled like a New York subway station. I suggested opening a window, but he refused, compromising only on pulling back his bedroom blackout curtains, which he had installed for his policeman hours.

He crawled into bed. Sweet Pea lighted beside him.

"Do you have fever?"

He shrugged.

I located a thermometer in the master bathroom's medicine chest, returned to the bedroom with it and shoved it under his tongue. It beeped, indicating a temperature of a hundred one.

"Have you called the doctor?"

His lips parted in his version of a smile. "How's a matchmaker like a Jewish mother?"

I braced myself for the joke. "I wouldn't know."

His smile stretched to a grin. "They both insist on chicken soup."

"I told you to get a flu shot."

He closed his eyes to half-mast.

I sat down on the edge of the bed and turned toward him. "Did you happen to see the coroner's reports on Fong Arroyo or Alexis Grand?"

His lids fluttered open. "What if I did?"

"Can you get me a copy?"

"None of your business," he muttered.

"C'mon, they were my clients."

"Why? Are you worried about whether her purse matched his?"

"Don't be a smart-ass."

He snickered, conveying enjoyment at getting a rise out of me.

"Someone put a snake in my glove compartment."

He ran his fingers through Sweet Pea's curls. "You sure have been seeing a lot of them lately." Larry's eyes glinted with skepticism. "Did anyone else see it?"

"Not that I know of."

He hesitated. "Then there's an argument to be made for it not being real, and if it isn't, maybe you should look into getting some help."

I raised the soup can in the air, ready to hurl it at him.

He flinched. "On the other hand, if it is real and somebody is trying to send you a message, you'd better listen."

"Forget it." I tossed the can on the bed and started to leave.

"Yeah, but I'm a little bit concerned after all these times. Chloe?"

I glanced back at him. "What is it?"

He picked up the can and shook it idly. "No more snakes."

CHAPTER 20

"SOMETIMES A PIZZA IS MORE THAN A PIE."

-- The Matchmaker's Bible

F orget depending on Larry for the autopsy reports. I
knew what I had to do. I had to make more of an effort to smoke out the murderer on my own. I fantasized
about marching around town in a cobra mask. Nobody
would think twice about it in L.A., where costumes were
an everyday occurrence on film sets and street corners.
Nobody, except the killer. Get a grip. Maybe it was time
for another tweet. I entered my office and continued to
my desk, considering what I wanted to say.

A page spewed from my fax machine. Well, now, what did we have here? I drifted over to the fax machine to have a look-see. A cover sheet for the autopsy reports materialized in Larry's scrawl. He must be feeling better. I waited for the rest of the pages to grind out, pleased the old boy had risen to the occasion, despite his protests less than twenty-four hours ago. I strolled over to my chair, plopped down in it and began to read the medical examiner's findings.

The documents confirmed Fong and Alexis had been strangled. Uneven pressure marks on the victims' necks indicated that a left-handed perp, not a snake, had killed them. The reports identified scratches and abrasions on both bodies, a contusion on Fong's abdomen, which appeared to have originated from a boa's squeeze, and traces of semen in Alexis' vagina. Holy shit. Had Tony Hammond cheated on Jill with her ex-husband? This would take transgenderism to another power. Which power?

In addition, the ME noted the presence of dark brown hairs embedded under the victims' fingernails and black nylon and tan wool fibers on each corpse. With the understaffing of crime labs today, a DNA analysis could take months. I couldn't afford to wait.

I attempted to profile the killer on a notepad. Left-handed, brown-haired man, wearing something black and tan, given to tweeting, snakes and sex with transsexuals, unless Alexis had slept with somebody else before her offing. My intuition told me he was probably from Alexis' social circle. I heard somebody in my lobby and stuffed everything in a drawer.

Zach filled the doorway with the aura of someone who had been chanting o*m*. "How was the rest of the wedding?" he asked in a congenial tone.

"Everything was fab, until I found a snake in my glove compartment."

"No."

"Yes."

"Did they catch the perp?"

"You mean psycho." I shook my head. "Not yet."

He frowned. "What about the snake?"

"I wouldn't know."

I invited him to sit.

He continued to stand. "It sure would be a waste of a beautiful woman if something were to happen to you."

I fidgeted with my hands. He was flirting with me again. In a past life, I had done a lot of flirting, had been quick to surrender to the journey, which kept leading to romantic relationships with the wrong men. That was then, before my estrogen began to wane, and I decided to stick to the personal intro biz and male friendships for fulfillment. I turned on my portable TV.

A cable station featured a tattoo convention at the Santa Monica Civic Auditorium. I winced as artists decorated flesh with dragons, cartoon characters and tribal images. Some of the clientele had enough piercings to set off a metal detector. Take the advice of a matchmaker, honey. Test drive before you buy. The camera cut to a bald-headed woman whose scalp resembled a flower garden, then pulled back to reveal Tony Hammond, inking a dahlia on her temple with his left hand. Lefty O'Toole, lefty President Obama, lefty Phil Mickelson, lefty the murderer. I switched off the TV, scooped up my purse and hiked it over my shoulder.

"Where are you going?"

"To a tattoo convention."

Zach jumped out of his chair. "I didn't realize you were the type."

"I think the killer's there."

"What gives you that impression?"

I mentioned Jill Grand's boyfriend, Tony Hammond.

"What do you intend to do about it?"

"Offer myself up as bait."

"Are you out of your mind?" His tone was a mixture of amusement and disbelief.

"I've tried everything else."

"You can't do that."

"I'm out of options."

"Are you some kind of idiot? Don't you think it's a tad risky?"

"I'm tired of trying to light a fire under the LAPD."

"Wait. I'm going with you." He grabbed my arm. "I insist upon going with you."

Zach wasn't exactly Mr. Universe. I gazed into his hazel eyes with uncertainty. He pulled out a broken board from his backpack.

"What's that?"

"Signed by my karate teacher after I split it in half."

"You don't say."

Zach was certainly full of surprises. I remembered how he had rescued me from a snake recently. I didn't want to take advantage of his good nature. He was my client. On the other hand, I wouldn't mind having company. Would I be encouraging his advances? I knew how to set limits; it was part of the job requirements. Besides, it wouldn't hurt to have a karate champ for backup.

The hum of stain guns buzzed through the Santa Monica Civic Auditorium. We maneuvered through yards of exposed flesh sporting colorful images, passing booths with do-it-yourself supplies, temporary tattoos and clothing designed to accentuate body art.

Tony Hammond operated under a sign that said SWEET PAIN OF VENICE. His tattooed deltoids spilled out of a sleeveless T-shirt. I waited for him to complete

Charles Manson's face across another man's pecs, while Zach surveyed sample designs taped to the booth.

"Doesn't that hurt?"

Tony scowled at me. "No more than pulling off a scab."

"Where'd you learn to do it?"

"At an art school in the country."

It sounded more like up the river to me. I mentioned I'd seen him on television.

"La-dee-da." He removed his plastic gloves with authority and glanced at me. "You're next."

Ignoring him, I said, "You appeared to be in a hurry the other day."

"I'm a busy man." He tossed the gloves in the trash.

"Was Fong Arroyo looking for a tattoo?"

"He was until somebody got to him."

"I thought Muslims don't get tattooed."

He studied me a few beats.

"What about Alexis Grand?"

"They were planning to have the same design," he said with an edge.

"How friendly were you with Alexis?"

"What business is it of yours?"

"What were you doing at her house?"

"You ought to stick to your matchmaking, Ms. Junior Cop. Do you want a tattoo or not?" He pressed his lips together in a straight line.

Zach rushed over to us, ready to intervene.

"How about a boa?" Pause. Breathe.

Tony picked up a marking pen, drew a quick sketch on a tablet and showed it to me. "How's this?"

I deliberated a moment. "Can you make the fangs a little bigger?"

Tony added a few more strokes.

I elbowed Zach. "Don't you think those are too big?"

He nodded vehemently.

Tony threw down his pen. "You're really beginning to piss me off."

"On second thought, I think I'll start with a temporary tattoo."

I reached for a Sweet Pain of Venice brochure, deposited it in my purse for future reference and seized Zach's arm. Catching a whiff of his leather jacket, I dragged him toward an exit.

Zach jerked his arm away. "I wonder how long it'll take for him to come after us."

"Aren't you a karate champ?"

He gave my elbow a squeeze and glanced over his shoulder. "What convinced you Tony Hammond's a murderer?"

"According to the autopsy reports..."

Zach's eyes challenged mine. "How'd you manage to lay your hands on those?"

"It wasn't easy." I focused on the steady stream of people coursing around us.

"What else did you learn?"

I told him about the dark brown hair strands, black and tan fibers and semen noted by the ME.

"Semen? Whose?"

"It'll take awhile for the DNA to come back."

"Crimes of passion?"

"Go figure what a guy with tattoos and dresses might be thinking."

The early evening air felt nippy. I buttoned my cardigan and swept through the parking lot with Zach, catching a whiff of his leather jacket. At the sound of footsteps, I checked my wake to make sure Tony wasn't following us. A pair of women lagged behind us, comparing their tattoos.

Satisfied, I turned back to Zach and said, "He's quite a piece of work, that Tony Hammond. I just wish his hair were a darker shade of brown."

"You still have your doubts about him."

I grew silent.

His gaze met mine. "I wouldn't mind having a look at the autopsy reports."

"Sorry, I don't think my ex would appreciate it."

"Why does he have to know?"

"What difference does it make to you?"

He shrugged. "I sell books. If I ever decide to write a mystery one day--"

"Just the same."

I came to a halt next to my rear bumper. "Mind taking a ride to the Valley with me?"

"Mind? Why would I mind, if it gives me more time with you?"

An hour later, I brought the car to a stop at the Encino home Jill shared with her son. Dusk silhouetted a stack of cartons on the porch.

"Spring cleaning day?" Zach quipped.

"I wonder if there's trouble in paradise."

I parked under a street lamp, left Zach in charge of lookout duty, then trekked up the path to the front door. Jill's collection of birds inside the house were engaged in shrill competition with the wild ones in the neighborhood. Circumventing the boxes, I made my way to her door and knocked.

Jill answered, wearing a pair of oversized sunglasses, which struck me as odd, given the time of day.

I lowered my gaze to a PC spilling out of one of the cartons of clothing, bedding and electronic equipment. "Is somebody moving?"

"I'm not."

"What about your boyfriend?"

"I'm through with men."

Where had I heard that line before?

She removed her glasses, revealing a shiner under her right eye.

"Wow. What happened to you?"

She averted her eyes from mine. "I just want him out of my life."

"Have you reported him?"

She shook her head. "I can handle it."

"I wonder what else he's capable of."

"I wouldn't put anything past Tony Hammond."

I waited for her to elaborate, but she didn't.

"These things tend to get worse over time, you know."

Ethan surfaced in the doorway, panting. "Mom, I can't find Pretzel. I can't find my cell phone either."

Zach met me on the sidewalk with a questioning look.

"Tony seems to have quite a left hook," I said.

Zach returned his cell phone to his belt case. "I've been telling you to lay off of him."

I hesitated. "I can't. I'm in too deep for that."

"I hope you don't get us killed."

The automatic sprinklers went on, spraying us with a steady stream of water. We hopscotched around them to my Saab. I started up the engine, made a Uee and headed toward the Ventura Freeway.

Zach brushed off the drops on his sleeves. A protracted silence followed. I neared a yellow light and slowed down, unwilling to chance a three-hundred-fifty-dollar ticket.

Zach consulted his watch. "I wish I didn't have to get back to the bookstore."

"That's all right. I intend to hole up with a pizza and my watchdog for the night."

Before delivering Zach to his car, I picked up Sweet Pea. Larry came to his door unshaven and still in his pajamas. The house smelled gamy and felt warm. Sweet Pea bared her teeth at Zach.

"Cool it," Larry said, grabbing her by the collar.

I introduced him to Zach.

Zach said with an amused expression, "Someone ought to teach her the downward dog position."

Larry scowled at him. "Do you expect her to see a Buddhist priest, too?"

Zach's smile evaporated. "It was just a suggestion."

"Lighten up, Larry."

"Yoga, schmoga," he muttered.

"Did you have your soup?" I asked in a chirpy voice meant to diffuse his hostility.

"Not yet."

I entered the house and made my way to his kitchen, then reached inside a cupboard for a saucepan and pulled out a scratched pot that belonged to both of us once upon a time.

Zach excused himself to use the john.

Larry said in a congested voice, "Is that your new boyfriend?"

"Don't be silly."

Larry coughed. "You seemed pretty cozy."

"He's a client."

"You ought to watch who you're keeping company with."

"I'm not worried."

"Yeah?"

"Yeah."

"Your dog doesn't like him, either."

I smiled wickedly. "You're jealous."

"Me, jealous? Don't flatter yourself."

Was my wusband jealous? He tended to be suspicious, which had served him well as a cop, if not in his personal life. At least Zach had been a good sport about Larry's prickliness. I dropped him off and headed home for the evening.

Close to seven p.m., I sat at the kitchen table looking over an assortment of takeout menus, trying to decide what to eat for dinner. Sweet Pea was no fan of Indian, Asian or Mexican, and we'd split a turkey burger the night before. At the end of the day, I called California Pizza Kitchen, ordered a chicken-rosemary special and told the young lady to skip the cheese. I took a quick trip to the mailbox and found a realtor's solicitation, bargain cruise announcement, PennySaver and another letter from the IRS waiting for me. What did we have here? I tore open the Department of Treasury's envelope and learned the IRS was billing me for back interest and penalties. Marvin was right. The IRS followed a person to the grave and beyond. There was no point in trying to work out a deal with Hank Buyers, not after the way he blamed me for his Edsel blowing up. I marched into the house and upstairs.

The doorbell rang and Sweet Pea barked. The Takeout Taxi people were quick on the draw for a change. I reached for my purse, hurried downstairs and yanked open the door. Someone wearing a mask with fangs pushed me inside and lunged for my neck.

CHAPTER 21

"NO GOOD DEED GOES UNPUNISHED."

-- *The Matchmaker's Bible*

I tried to fend off my attacker, but he had strong hands. I felt the air whoosh out of me. My head grew light and my arms flailed out. Sweet Pea growled and sank her teeth into his leg. At-a-girl. Way to go. My assailant kicked my dog across the hardwood floor while still holding on to my neck. I heard her whimper and attempted to wiggle free. He tightened his hold on my neck. The room swam in slow motion.

A tentative male voice said in a far away tone, "Takeout Taxi."

My assailant let go of my neck and rushed out the door. I sucked in air, unable to take in enough oxygen. My breath came out in jagged gasps. Sweet Pea looked at me with a dazed expression. I stumbled over to her and ran my fingers over her body, trying to identify the painful spots. She didn't cry out. She stood up for a moment, then sat right down again, unable to remain on all fours. I sprang to my feet. My watch said six thirty. Never mind animal ER was no match for a regular veterinarian. It was the only game now.

The Takeout Taxi kid returned holding a glove, tan like the fibers noted in the autopsy reports. The glove was too big for my hands but ought to fit a man's.

Shaking the glove at me, the kid said, "Woulda had him in four, killed him in five, if it wasn't for the pizza." The thickness of his glasses magnified his pale blue eyes and lashes, like a microscope. He gestured to the hot box. "Where do you want the pizza?"

"The pizza. Yes, the pizza."

I made room on the credenza mechanically. He unzipped the hot box. The fragrance of garlic and rosemary escaped from it but neglected to tempt me.

He removed the California Pizza Kitchen box and set it down. "Did he take anything?"

"That was no burglar," I said in a tinny voice. "Murder interruptus."

A distasteful expression spread across his lips. "Guess I did a good deed, then."

"I'll say."

He presented the glove to me. "People at work are going to be calling, wondering where I am."

I cast the glove aside and fumbled for the wallet in my purse. I had enough cash to pay the bill but used my American Express, so I could add a twenty-five-dollar tip. Under the circumstances, the gratuity was a bargain. I shoved the box at him.

"Do me a favor. Take the pizza, too."

He shook his head. "Thanks. I'm trying to quit."

"Do you have a card?"

"For Overeaters Anonymous?"

"The police. I'm sure they'll want to talk to you."

"Yeah, sure, lady. He reached into his jacket pocket and retrieved a Takeout Taxi one.

"What's *your* name?"

"Jared. I'm the only Jared there."

"Well, you take care now, you hear?" He lingered a moment and opened his mouth, as if he wanted to say something before he left but didn't.

I closed the door behind him. A gust of cool air blew in. I shivered, but it wasn't from the temperature; of that I was sure. I grabbed the phone and called the LAPD, figuring I ought to have enough credibility with the cops by now.

The closest animal ER was located on Sepulveda Boulevard, which pet owners referred to as veterinary row because of the abundance of dog and cat hospitals along the street. I sped there with Sweet Pea and found the lot full of cars.

Mother told me I should have married a doctor. She was wrong. I should have married a veterinarian. Unlike physicians, animal doctors collected their fees up front and didn't have to worry about insurance payments or malpractice suits. My epiphany was too late for me but not for my By Invitation Only customers.

I parked underground on the bottom level, pulled out some business cards (the visit shouldn't be a total loss) and hauled Sweet Pea upstairs.

A group of people who appeared to be related because of their long faces hogged the chairs in the waiting room. I caught a whiff of urine mixed with wet dog. My stomach did a flip-flop. As I charged over to the desk, I breathed through my mouth. Speaking above a chorus of barks, meows and whines, I checked in with a sloe-eyed receptionist.

She told me all the rooms were busy but offered to take Sweet Pea in back. I handed over my dog, anxious to speed up the process, and returned to the waiting room. The sound of tears and angry voices turned my attention to the people with long faces who were arguing about whether their cat had tennis elbow or not. Although it didn't play tennis, it chased the balls.

One thing was certain--none of them was about to offer me a seat. The receptionist called me to the window and asked if I would consent to x-rays and blood work. Was there a question? I gave my permission. My cell phone rang. I dug into my purse for my BlackBerry, recognized Larry's number on its readout panel and answered.

"What the hell happened? Are you okay?"

"I think so." I could hear an old *Dragnet* episode playing in the background.

"How's the dog?"

"I'm waiting to speak to the vet."

The TV episode sounded like "Death on a Merry-Go-Round." I had watched it enough times with him to recognize the dialogue.

"Where are you? I'll be right over."

I paced back and forth in the lobby. How difficult would it be for Tony Hammond to leave the Santa Monica auditorium at five p.m., throw on a snake costume and arrive in Playa del Rey by seven p.m.? He even had time for an In-N-Out burger. Never mind his light brown hair.

Larry surfaced in the waiting room, looking as if he'd shed a few pounds. He drew his lips back in a smile and marched over to me with a contrite air.

"You must be pretty shaken up. Do you need to see a doctor?" He buzzed around me like a mosquito.

I shook my head, savoring his solicitousness. Too bad it came a day late and dollar short.

"How's the dog?"

"I don't know."

"Let me handle it," he said in an apparent attempt to redeem himself for giving me a hard time.

I raised my arms in surrender. "Go to it, Lorenzo."

He threaded past me to the reception window and identified himself as Detective Larry Chellini.

"What are you investigating?" the sloe-eyed receptionist asked.

"My dog Sweet Pea."

She studied him a moment. "Is this personal or professional?"

"What's the difference? I want to speak to her veterinarian."

The receptionist said over her shoulder, "There's a detective here who wants to speak to Sweet Pea's veterinarian."

Larry corrected her. "*Homicide* detective."

The family of long faces got up to retrieve their cat, leaving plenty of Eames-style chairs available. I settled into a red vinyl one, but jumped up as soon as a woman in scrubs who looked as if she were playing hookey from junior high school appeared in the lobby with Sweet Pea. I stepped over to her with Larry.

She greeted us with a grave expression. "Your dog appears to have a concussion. I'd like to keep her overnight to do some additional tests."

The back of my throat closed.

"Tests?" said Larry.

"MRI, urine, fecal."

He winced. "Would you mind throwing in a set of steak knives?"

The veterinarian smiled as if she had been down the same road before. "You don't have to do everything."

What did she care? It wasn't her dog. Forget soliciting her as a client. I tossed my business card back into my purse, deciding to give it to somebody else. Larry asked for a cost breakdown.

I gave him a sharp glance. "That won't be necessary."

"Oh, yeah? I thought we have joint custody."

"Don't mind him," I said, taking the reigns from the dickhead. "Do whatever you have to."

Larry followed me to my townhouse. The street light illuminated Lyons, Garcia and a couple of other cops lingering outside my entrance with flashlights. An elderly couple appeared to have interrupted their stroll to take in the excitement around my unit.

I maneuvered into my garage and felt an odd tingling down one side of my neck, which I attributed to post-traumatic stress. I didn't pick up on Larry parking in his former space until he was next to me.

"Make yourself at home."

He eased out of his Explorer, reached in back and removed an overnight bag. "Fresh shirt, change of underwear and razor. Tools of the trade."

"What gives you the idea you're staying?"

"Don't worry. It's strictly professional. I'll sleep in the guest room."

The good news was I didn't have to worry about my safety. The bad news was it was too late to call an alarm company. The automatic light went off in the garage. I got out of the car, shut the garage door and scrambled upstairs to let in the others.

Larry said, "Whoa. Something smells good. What's for dinner?"

I glanced over my shoulder. "Cold pizza."

"I love cold pizza almost as much as cold Pad Thai. What kind is it?"

"Chicken rosemary."

He said in a sulky tone, "Why'd you have to order the chicken?"

"Some of us are still carnivores. You'll have to eat around it."

Larry continued to occupy himself with the pizza while I switched on the porch light and unlocked the patio door for the other cops. Lyons introduced me to Franklin, the same forensic guy I'd seen at Alexis' house but hadn't met at the time.

Franklin asked if I knew anybody who wore a size eleven Nike running shoe.

"I don't think so." I added, "It didn't occur to me to look at the killer's feet."

Franklin tugged on the small silver hoop in his earlobe. "How about a size nine Ecco shoe?"

"One of the prints just might belong to the Takeout Taxi kid." I located his business card in my purse and thrust it in Franklin's hand.

Garcia hesitated before entering. "Any snakes in there?"

I assured him there weren't. He projected a relieved air and sauntered inside with Lyons and a pair of patrol officers, whose badges indicated they were in training. Franklin wandered onto the patio by himself.

Garcia was quick to tell me how the boa in my glove compartment was now in custody.

"I'm so glad."

"Me, too."

Lyons gave him an odd look.

Franklin asked me to step outside with him for a moment. I joined him in anticipation of a new development.

He said in a halting cadence, "I understand you arrange discreet meetings." His hand gravitated to his earring, as if to make sure it were still there.

"Does this have something to do with one of my clients?"

He let go of his earring and lowered his hand to his side. "This is a personal matter."

I gave a mini exhale, starting to catch his drift. The night air smelled of jasmine.

"It's difficult, with my hours and all, for me to meet women." His gaze swept across the sliding glass door separating the living room from the patio. "The thing is, I'm a very private person."

"I understand. Give me a jingle." I rattled off By Invitation Only's telephone number, which he transferred to his smart phone. "By the way, I offer a discount to anyone in law enforcement."

He smiled with interest. "How much?"

"Ten percent."

"All the better."

I pumped the air with my fist.

Larry glided through the sliding-glass door, waving a pizza wedge at us. "Anyone hungry?"

"No, thanks," Franklin said.

I shook my head, annoyed at the interruption.

Larry said with a nosy expression, "What have you two been up to?"

I wasn't about to betray Franklin's confidence, so I mentioned the tan glove in my living room credenza and led them to it.

Franklin picked up the glove with a pair of tweezers, deposited it in an official baggie and labeled it with a Sharpie, while Lyons, Garcia and the pair of rookies looked on with interest. Not Larry. Preoccupied with his stomach, he discarded the chicken pieces from his slice of pizza on a napkin before he dug in.

"There ought to be enough DNA cells on this little goody to implicate somebody," Franklin said in a pleased tone.

I dropped down on the sectional, hoping he was right. Garcia sent the pair of rookies outside to look for witnesses, while Lyons eased next to me on the couch. He offered me an Altoid. The flavor of apples exploded on my tongue. He helped himself to an Altoid and asked me to describe my attacker.

"Let's see--he was average sized, and he had strong hands, even with a pair of gloves on, and he was wearing a black track suit and a mask with fangs."

"Did he say anything?"

I shook my head. "Nothing. If only Tony Hammond had darker hair..."

"You saw his hair?"

I felt Larry's eyes on me, which triggered a warning vibe.

"Yes," I fibbed.

Larry shuffled to the bar, uncorked a bottle of wine and handed me a glass of something red, which appeared to be my reward for being a good girl and keeping my mouth shut about the autopsy reports. "You look as if you can use this."

"Did you open a new bottle?"

"Why?"

"Because I was saving it."

"For what?"

The phone rang.

Lyons reached for it. "Detective Lyons."

Silence.

He handed me the receiver.

I mouthed the words, "Who is it?"

Lyons didn't answer. Larry rushed upstairs, in an apparent effort to listen to the conversation on an extension.

I lifted the receiver to my ear. "Hello."

Zach said in a concerned voice, "What are the cops doing there?"

I briefed him about my intruder.

"What kind of person would hurt an innocent dog?" Without waiting for an answer, he added, "I had a feeling something like this was going to happen. Let the police handle it, all of it."

I took a sip of wine. It's full-bodied flavor told me it was a cabernet sauvignon and gave me a warm glow. I cupped the goblet in my hands and watched the light bounce off the rim. While tempted to invite Zach over, I decided against it, unwilling to subject him to any more crap from Larry.

"I've got to go," I said.

"Are you having pizza with them?"

CHAPTER 22
"LOVE AND JUSTICE ARE BLIND."
-- *The Matchmaker's Bible*

I tightened my grip on the phone. "How'd you know about the pizza, Zach?"

"Don't you remember telling me about your plans to order in?"

I put down the wineglass in my other hand and rubbed the bridge of my nose, realizing he was right.

Zach said, "Is there somebody else on the line?"

"Who is this?" Larry asked.

Zach introduced himself.

"Is he the same character you were with this afternoon?" I cut in. "What of it?"

"He has your home phone number?" Larry groaned. "And I suppose he has your address, too."

"You don't have to worry about Zach."

"I'd better get back to work," Zach said awkwardly.

Moments later, Larry bounded downstairs. "What's he bothering you at home for, Chloe?"

"He wasn't bothering me. He was bothering you. Zach's been at the bookstore all evening."

"How do you know where he's been?"

"Press star sixty-nine. Trace the call."

"Did you introduce him to Fong Arroyo and Alexis Grand?"

"No, he never met either one of them."

Garcia came in from the patio with a triumphant flicker in his eyes. "I found the owner of the size-nine shoe."

Lyons leaned forward on the sectional. "The pizza kid?"

Garcia nodded.

"What about the other print?"

"We're still working on it."

"What else did the pizza kid say?"

"The suspect's Caucasian."

"The pizza kid saw his face?"

Garcia shook his head. "Only his hand when the glove came off."

Lyons and Garcia were first to leave my house.

Franklin glanced at his watch. "I ought to be home in time for *CSI*. The consultant was one of us, you know. Now she's making the big bucks."

"Maybe she can land you a job."

"I wish," he said with an envious note.

I took him aside, hoping a new honey would suffice as a consolation prize. "Don't forget to call." I fished out a By Invitation Only card from my jacket pocket, thrust it in Franklin's hand and escorted him to the door.

Yawning, I started upstairs. Larry asked to borrow my toothpaste since he had run out of his. I grabbed an extra tube of Colgate Total from the master bathroom and presented it to him.

"Be sure to squeeze from the bottom."

"I always loved your bottom." A naughty smile played on his lips. "Would you like me to tuck you in?"

"No, thanks."

He touched my cheek.

"You promised to behave."

"I lied." His cornflower-blue eyes shone with confidence.

Never mind the bad-boy charm. I was unable to shake the baggage of too much history between us. If I wanted somebody to tuck me in, it wouldn't be him. What about Zach? He was in my thoughts a lot lately.

"Goodnight, Larry."

A knock on the door woke me. The room was dark. I sat upright in bed and checked the clock. It was barely six forty-five. I shut my eyes.

Larry said, "Rise and shine. Do you want your coffee?"

I stretched. "Must you be so cheerful in the morning?"

He entered, dressed for the day in a pair of chinos, sport shirt and sneakers and smelling like talcum powder.

I laced my fingers around the coffee mug and looked up at him. "We'd better call the hospital."

"I already have. Sweet Pea can go home."

I raised the mug to my lips while the steam escaped from the top. "Aren't you Johnny on the spot?"

"You never appreciated me," he said tongue-in-cheek.

He was still such a pro at stirring up the guilt. I took a swig, figuring there were no victims in this world--only volunteers. The decaf tasted strong and burned my tongue. I rested the mug on the nightstand, which clattered on the wood. As I consulted my BlackBerry, I noticed the Chamber of Commerce golf tournament on my calendar. I broke the news to Larry.

"Don't cancel."

"You're the last person I expected to hear this from."

"The murderer isn't a marksman. You'll be fine. Besides, I'll be your caddy."

I stared at him. "You?"

"Why not?"

"You don't know the difference between a nine iron and pitching wedge."

"What's the big deal?"

"There are no caddies."

"I'll watch from the gallery."

"You think this is a PGA tour?"

On the way to the tournament, we made a detour to the animal ER. Sweet Pea's bill came to eighteen hundred dollars and fifty-three cents. Larry shook his head in dismay and reached for his wallet. In my compromised financial state, I waited him out.

He leaned against the counter, studying me with anticipation. "Where's your part, kiddo?"

I snapped my fingers. "I was afraid you'd say that." Pause. "How about if I take care of the fifty-three cents?"

He thumped me on the shoulder. "You were the one who wanted joint custody."

I shrugged. "Yesterday you were worried about me dying."

"That was yesterday."

The aroma of disinfectant reached my nostrils. I glanced at a tech wiping up a puddle of urine on the linoleum floor.

My gaze shifted to Larry's face. "Ninety percent of the time she's with me, you know."

"You expect me to amortize it?"

Sweet Pea's soprano rang out from the chorus of barks behind the hospital doors, which indicated she recognized our voices and wanted out of there. Why prolong it?

"My Visa's maxed out."

"Don't you have any other cards?"

I ripped out three others. "These, too."

"You never could stick to a budget."

"Things have been a little dicey lately."

"Whose fault is that?"

"Be nice."

Larry jiggled his foot. "I ought to let them make chopped meat out of her."

"Don't joke."

His lips parted in a bad-boy smile. "Who's joking?"

I addressed the cashier, whose sunburned nose was in process of peeling. "Would you mind billing me for my half?"

Larry sighed with resignation. "Give me your fifty-three fucking cents. I'll take care of the rest of it this one time."

Sweet Pea's tests showed no internal bleeding, only a mild concussion. Mild, schmild. I was tempted to ram a golf ball down the perp's throat. For all I knew, he was dusting off his golf clubs about now. Contrary to what Larry had said, was I to be Snake Man's hole in one? I preferred to make him mine. How would my nemesis know where I'd be? I hadn't told anyone but Larry.

A tech handed Sweet Pea to me. I cradled her in my arms. Since Larry and I had driven in separate cars, I carried Sweet Pea to mine and followed Larry to his house, where we dropped off his Explorer and the dog. We left her there to recuperate and continued to the golf course in my Saab because it contained my clubs.

I'd put away my irons and woods after Fong was murdered. Accustomed to spending a couple of hours practicing at the driving range before a tournament, I hoped I wouldn't embarrass myself out there. On a good day, I had yet to break a hundred. On a bad day, all bets were off. At least I wasn't competing for money. That said, I wouldn't mind landing a new client or two. Sometimes, when I laid off the game for a couple of weeks, I actually shot a better score. Go figure the *g* word.

The Manhattan Beach executive course backed up to a Marriott hotel and gated residential community. I swung into the course's parking lot and surveyed the cars. None of them looked familiar. I chose a spot next to a pair of women changing into street shoes beside an open trunk. Apparently, they were finished for the day, although I was just beginning. My stomach knotted like yarn. I eyed my watch. Realizing I had less than a half hour to warm up my short and long games before the tournament, I slid out of the car. An ocean breeze kicked up, contributing to my nervousness. Larry lifted my clubs out of the trunk and grabbed a book of Sudoku puzzles for himself, which he tucked underarm. He suggested I keep my cell phone with me in case of an emergency. I slipped it in my golf bag and tugged my equipment over to the putting green, where I parted company with Larry, who retreated to the clubhouse.

I tapped and pitched balls into cups, keeping an eye out for a suspicious face. Maybe Larry was right. A golf tournament wasn't the place for a strangler. I purchased a small bucket of balls and practiced with my irons and woods on the driving range. I managed to hook or slice every other shot, an ominous sign.

At check-in time, I wheeled my golf bag over to the registration table. With my strokes were already in place, I focused on clearing my head of extraneous negative thoughts and getting in touch with my killer instinct.

A familiar ponytail peeked out of a man's cap as he stood in line. Was I dreaming? Zach hadn't mentioned he was a golfer. From several yards away, I recognized his contagious laugh.

I blinked. "Zach?"

He whipped around and said with a sly smile, "Who else?"

I fixed my gaze on his Callaways. "I had no idea you play golf."

He chuckled. "There's a lot about me you don't know, Ms. Matchmaker. We both play golf, we're single, we enjoy merlot wine. We're ninety-five percent a match, which is off the charts."

I glanced at him curiously. "What about the other five percent?"

"You'll have to find out for yourself."

"You don't quit." I gestured to his TaylorMade driver. "How do you like it?"

"It's given me ten extra yards on my tee shots."

"I wouldn't mind the extra distance."

He handed me the club. "Try it."

I moved away and took a couple of swings.

"You ought to treat yourself."

I returned the club to him. "At the moment, I have other priorities."

"I'll bet. What happened after I spoke to you last night?"

I told him about the left-handed glove and size-eleven footprint.

"Any suspects?"

I shrugged. "Not that I'm aware of."

My foursome included a couple of computer nerds with range finders on their belts and a man who walked as if he were in the early stages of Parkinson's disease. I was glad Zach wasn't among them. For all I knew, he was a scratch golfer. The man who moved with jerking motions set up his first shot. He took a practice swing, addressed the ball and connected in some kind of strange dance.

"Fore," he shouted.

I ducked.

Someone yelled, "Ouch."

I glanced up. Larry was on the ground, no more than ten yards away, holding his arm. I rushed over to him.

"Are you hurt?"

He continued to favor his arm. "It's broken. I'm sure it's broken."

"What the hell are you doing out here?"

The man apologized to Larry, attributing his hook shot to a scratchy sweater. He said in an embarrassed tone, "You've got to watch out for those hidden menaces."

Of all the lame excuses. I helped Larry to his feet.

"You didn't answer your cell phone." He eyed me with a dazed expression.

"I was in a tournament. Besides, I didn't hear it."

"Are you deaf?"

"I forgot to charge it last night."

"I tried to catch you before you teed off. I just got a call from Garcia. Your buddy Tony and his girlfriend must have kissed and made up. She insists he was with her the whole evening."

"When?"

"From six o'clock on."

"That's a lie."

"How do you know?"

"I was there."

"The whole time?"

"Part of it."

Jill had been quick to implicate Tony when I saw her last. She'd made it clear she wanted him out of her life, the way I wanted the murderer out of mine. What had changed her mind? Could she be that desperate for a lube from a grease ball?

I rode back to the first-aid station with Larry and the marshal. The nurse decided my wusband had a bone bruise and gave him an ice pack and couple of Advil. Larry insisted upon an x-ray. So much for the tournament. At least the awards banquet was still an option. I looked forward to finishing up with Larry in time to catch up with Zach and the others at the Chamber of Commerce luncheon.

Larry and I sped down Sepulveda to the nearest urgent-care center.

I said under my breath, "I don't understand."

"What don't you understand?"

"Jill Grand's about-face."

"Is there something you know that the cops don't?"

"She was alone when I left her."

"So? Maybe her boyfriend came home afterward."

"I don't know about that."

"If Lyons and Garcia are satisfied..."

I took my eyes off the road long enough to focus on his face in repose. "It's not their lives, bubula."

"Don't you think they checked her story?"

"They didn't consult me."

"For God's sake, give them some credit."

Later, the urgent-care doctor confirmed that Larry had nothing broken-and sent him home with his arm in a sling. Unable to decide which hurt more, his arm or his bruised ego, I dropped him off to recuperate with Sweet Pea.

My watch said one thirty, too late for the Chamber of Commerce awards luncheon. I settled for a peanut butter Balance bar from a local 7-Eleven and polished it off quickly. Never mind it tasted stale. I was hungry. I crumpled up the wrapper and phoned Jill Grand from the parking lot.

She said hollowly, "I guess I exaggerated a bit. I'm sorry I made such a fuss. Tony and I had a little misunderstanding and I overreacted."

"But your eye--"

"I slipped. It was an accident."

Ethan shouted in the background, "Why don't you tell the truth? Shit, Ma. There you go again."

"Watch your language, Ethan. I'll be off in a minute." She continued with a nervous laugh, "Boyfriends come and go, but kids--"

"Boyfriends with size-eleven feet?"

"Where'd you get that idea?" She hesitated. "Actually, my son's the one with the size-elevens."

CHAPTER 23
"DON'T GET MAD, GET EVEN."

-- The Matchmaker's Bible

I glanced at the dashboard and attempted to organize my thoughts. Did Ethan own a pair of Nikes in size eleven? I wasn't about to ask his loose-cannon mother the question. Ethan had worn sneakers when I first met him, although I hadn't paid attention to what kind. After the way he chewed me out for wearing leather shoes, his must have consisted of something else. I took out my phone and Googled Nike footwear for men. Most of the styles featured fabric uppers and

244

rubber soles, satisfying his no-leather requirement. Okay, so how prevalent were size-eleven feet? According to another Google site I checked, size eleven was the most common one for males in this country, although at the time of the American Revolution, it was only six, which gave Big Foot a whole new meaning. Next question: Was Ethan left-handed like the murderer? I started the engine and maneuvered my car into the right lane. My Bluetooth alerted me to a call, which I answered quickly.

Zach said in a perplexed tone, "Where'd you go? I saved you a seat at the luncheon."

I told him about Larry's accident.

"Now that you mention it, I heard something about a guy getting hit by a golf ball."

"That was him."

I commented on my recent conversation with Jill.

"You think her son did it?"

"His shoe size matches, and he does have the right color hair."

"Wow, his father becomes a woman, and his mother takes up with a friggin' cross-dressing felon. That's enough to make anyone lose it."

Zach said something else, but I slammed on the brakes as a bus cut in front of me and had to ask him to repeat himself.

"You don't want to hear about my childhood, Chloe. Dysfunction with a capital D."

Who wasn't from dysfunction? My parents had been too busy listening to their needs to pay much attention to mine as a kid.

Zach suggested we talk more over a bite to eat. "On second thought," he said, "it's probably not a good idea for you to be running around to restaurants, unless your ex, the cop, will be with us."

"Forget Larry. He's at home nursing his wounds with his favorite dog."

"In that case, why don't I bring in something for dinner?" I sighed. "If it were anyone else, but you, Zach..."

He chuckled. "Six o'clock?"

I started to give him directions, but his voice broke up.

"Can you hear me?"

"Barely."

"Are you still..."

Silence.

The joy of cell phones. I felt as if I were playing a new reality game called Fill in the Electronic Blanks.

Zach showed up on time with a bottle of pinot grigio and enough food to feed a hockey team.

The aroma of ginger teased my nostrils. "Yum. What do we have here?" I poked my nose in the bags and looked at him quizzically.

He smiled a vulnerable smile. "I hope you like Asian fusion."

"Delice."

Zach set the bags on the kitchen counter and slung his leather jacket over a chair. "So what's this about Ethan Grand?"

Reiterating what I knew, I proceeded to transfer the sushi on to a serving platter with a pair of chopsticks. "I still have some doubts about Ethan. For one thing, does he own a pair of Nikes? For another, is he right or left-handed? Also, how's a fourteen-year-old kid supposed to haul himself around town with a snake, at all hours, on L.A.'s limited public transportation system?"

"Maybe he had some help."

I nodded. "Now that's a possibility."

Zach filched a piece of California roll from the sushi platter and popped it in his mouth. "Did you know Japanese food's an aphrodisiac?"

I laughed.

He leaned over me and touched my temple. "I'm serious."

Our eyes met and he pulled me toward him. His manly aroma was intoxicating. Wait just a second. What about the rules of *The Matchmaker's Bible*? And I hated ponytails on men. Zach kissed me and I kissed back, enjoying his lips on mine. I dropped the chopsticks, which clicked on the kitchen tiles. After all these years, who knew a man's stubble could feel this good against my cheek? He tasted like crab and avocado. Suddenly, his shirt buttons cut into my flesh and I pulled away.

"What's wrong?"

"Smushed sushi."

"What's that supposed to mean?"

My excuse sounded as lame to me as the Chamber of Commerce golfer's when he'd blamed his wild shot on a scratchy sweater.

"Let's eat."

As soon as Zach left, I fetched Sweet Pea from Larry's house. She climbed on my legs, squealing in the foyer.

He stared at me in the incandescent light. "You've been drinking."

"I had a glass of wine. Do you mind?"

"I can smell it on you." His eyes darkened. "Where have you been?"

"I had things to do."

He snickered. "You just got laid."

"What's the matter with you?"

He tilted his head. "I can see it all over you."

"You can?" I gave myself the once-over. "What do you see that I don't?"

He motioned to the door. "Just go and take your dog with you."

Later that night, I stretched across my bed with Sweet Pea and reviewed the night's events. Zach hadn't pushed things after dinner, and I couldn't decide whether I was happy or sad about it. I lay there taking in the faint light between the shutters and imagining his pleasant odor. Sweet Pea began to snore. I listened to the even rhythm of the sounds. What did Larry see on me that I didn't? At some point, I fell asleep.

The telephone woke me the next morning. I groped for my landline and heard dial tone. The sound continued. I leaped for my BlackBerry on the nightstand and tapped the talk button. Franklin wanted to get together that afternoon.

"Have there been any new developments with the DNA evidence?" I asked.

"It's still too early for that."

"Can't you speed things up?"

My question appeared to entertain him. "Everyone wants to step over everyone else in this game."

"Don't you have any clout?"

"You're competing with people who've been arrested and have court dates."

"Franklin, how do you expect me to find you a match if I'm dead?"

"You're better off talking to Lyons and Garcia. They'll be able to intervene with their commanding officer, if they think it's urgent enough."

"Never mind. How about lunch at Cafe Marina this afternoon?" I encouraged him to bring along photos of three of his exes.

"What good will that do?"

"Most people have a type, you know."

He whined, "I was married for twenty-three years and spent the last ten trying to forget them."

"All right. What about girlfriends?"

"That's why I'm consulting a matchmaker."

I hung up from Franklin, took his advice and texted Lyons about the DNA evidence. Afterward, I washed my face, tugged on a pair of sweats and led Sweet Pea into the morning chill.

The crows were having a hissy fit out there, which evoked the shrill sounds of Jill's birds. My thoughts shifted to her son, Ethan. Preferring to deal with him and not his mother, I coaxed Sweet Pea into the house, called Milliken Middle School, which he had mentioned attending, and made sure he was in class that day.

Café Marina overlooked Mother's Beach, a shallow stretch of sand and surf that catered to toddlers wading in the white water with their mommies and frolicking in the sand with pails and shovels.

Over poached salmon at one of the patio tables, Franklin said, "I just want a woman who knows who Simon and Garfunkel are." His eyes darted to the neighboring tables, as if worried somebody might overhear us.

I put down my fork, catching a whiff of fish. "You mean age appropriate."

The sun glinted on his silver hoop earring.

He nodded. "A woman in her early sixties or late fifties. No, maybe in her mid-fifties. Even fifty or..."

My phone chirped above the clink of dishes and voices.

"Excuse me," I said before Franklin changed his mind again.

I scrambled in my purse for my phone, grabbed it and tapped the answer key. Nathan, my producer client with a little p, claimed the zoo was having difficulty selecting a mate for its male gorilla.

"What does that have to do with me?"

"They've been borrowing females from everywhere. Got any tips?"

"Normally, I start with an interview and questionnaire," I said in a salty tone.

"What about body language?"

I hesitated. "You mean how they pound their heads and beat their chests?"

A perplexed expression played on Franklin's face.

Nathan said, "When can I send over a camera crew?"

"Is this some kind of joke?"

"There must be some rules that cross species. It's going to be great, just great. Fox loves the idea."

"From gorilla mating to *King Kong III.*"

"Okay, so it ain't a fifty million-dollar blockbuster, but it's a start and I've already raised the money. What do you say?"

"My minimum fee's five thousand up front, six for gorillas."

"No problem."

"No problem?"

"No problem."

Apparently, my producer with a little p had graduated to big P status. I let Franklin pick up the lunch tab, testing what kind of sport he would be with the ladies.

Opting for the indirect approach with a teenage suspect, I shot over to Snakes R Us, located on the corner of Lincoln and Pico, to pick up a present for Ethan. Although I contemplated buying a dozen doughnuts to determine if he was left-handed, after my conversation with Nathan, I felt flush enough to stick to the tried and true.

Advertisements for mice, reptile sand, scoopers, even birthday parties, blanketed the plate-glass windows of Snakes R Us. I wandered inside the Santa Monica store, which smelled pristine and had an eerie silence to it. Nobody else was around, except a salesman with a handlebar mustache. He leaned over the counter, smiling.

"You do birthday parties?" I asked.

He tweaked one side of his mustache. "We supply the reptiles. You furnish the cake."

"That sounds fair enough."

"Interested in one?"

I shook my head. "I'm interested in a garter snake."

"Not here, lady," he said in a condescending tone. "You can find those next door in the empty lot."

Unable to picture myself crawling around in the dirt wearing a pair of clean cords and shirt, I said, "How about a boa? Nothing big or expensive." I surveyed the cages stacked on shelves lining the walls. "Or anything that bites. Something that can be returned, if it's not right."

The salesman twisted both ends of his mustache. "How about a rubber belly?"

"What's that?"

"They're quite sweet boas. Normally, they cost seventy-five to two hundred fifty, but we have a special going on today."

"How much?"

"Only twenty-four, ninety-nine."

"Is it alive?"

"Of course it's alive. It even includes a container and light."

I showed up at Milliken Middle School that afternoon with a three-foot-long rubber belly in a container on the back seat of my Saab. Buses and cars flooded the surrounding streets like LAX on a Thanksgiving weekend. I wangled a spot several blocks away, opened the windows a crack so the snake wouldn't suffocate and locked the car. I planted myself next to the flagpole and waited for the dismissal bell to ring. In a previous incarnation, I had visited the school to check on a parolee. Worried I would die of a stroke from the job, I opened By Invitation Only. Now I feared succumbing to a fucking strangler.

Close to three o'clock, a handful of cops and faculty spread out in front of the Spanish revival building shaded by magnolia trees in bloom. At the sound of a bell, the front doors popped open, and a hoard of pushing, shoving adolescents spilled out in all directions, some carrying backpacks, others wheeling bookbags, all of whom shared one thing in common. They were at an age that was neither caterpillars, nor butterflies. A group of teachers followed them out, looking spent.

A familiar voice cracked behind me. "Hey, what are you doing here?"

I spun around and came face to face with Ethan. Instinctively, I glanced at his feet. His sneakers bore a Nike logo.

My gaze shifted to his. "I bought you a present."

His brown eyes measured mine. "What'd you do that for?"

"I wanted to." I invited him to come with me.

The crowd began to thin on a comfortable San Fernando Valley afternoon.

Ethan followed me to my parking spot, slouching under the weight of his backpack.

When we got to my car, he rested his head on a window and peered through the glass. "A terrarium?"

"Not just a terrarium."

"I don't see anything else."

I shoved him out of the way and stared at the empty tank with the lid ajar on the backseat of my car. Could the critter have crawled into the trunk or motor? What if it was in the carburetor? I feared a seven-hundred-dollar repair job.

"Where the hell's the snake?"

He squinted at me. "There's supposed to be a snake?"

I corrected him. "A rubber belly."

He giggled. "Cool."

Ethan opened the car door with his right hand.

I said, "You're right-handed?"

He swiveled around. "Aren't most people?"

Never mind his shoe size or the kind of sneakers he wore. His dominant hand was inconsistent with the pressure marks on the murder victims' necks, as described in the autopsy reports.

He dove inside the car and emerged with the ground-colored reptile, muttering something about it liking wheel wells because of their warmth. The thing coiled around his arm like a living tattoo.

"Can I have it?"

"Don't you think you'd better check with your mother first?"

"None of her beeswax."

"Just the same."

Ethan appeared to transcend this planet to another, perhaps a safer one ruled by animals. "Hey, you know how to tell the difference between a rubber boa and Mexican one?"

"By its Spanish accent?"

He giggled. "Hey, I like you." He gestured to the snake's head. "The Mexican one would never have scales this big."

I confiscated the rubber belly and restored it to the terrarium.

"Get in," I said.

I started the engine. "Does Tony still live with you?"

"I guess."

"I'm surprised after the way--"

"My mom's loco."

"What makes you say that?"

"She just is."

"I think he was in my neighborhood last night."

Ethan said in an indifferent tone, "Hey, can I turn on the radio?"

I preempted him, afraid of being blasted out of the car by a teenager, and tuned in a station featuring a Cold Play song.

> *You're in control,*
> *Is there anywhere*
> *You wanna go?*

How much was I in control? What about Tony Hammond? I drove on in silence. I made a left on Havenhurst and continued to the shabby Cape Cod that Ethan shared with his mother and her boyfriend. Several doors away, Ethan announced his mother was home. I took my eyes off the road long enough to see her in the doorway with a burly man. The bruiser had the same stringy hair and build as one of Juanita's henchmen. I winced at the thought of him twisting my ear again. No way was I about to let that happen.

I glanced at Ethan. "Who's that man?"

"I don't know."

"Have you seen him here before?"

"Uh-uh."

I navigated to the curb and stopped the car. Juanita had been trying to find Alexis' patent diary. Tony had been up to no good when I ran into him at Alexis' house. The interaction between Jill and the bruiser looked to be civil. Could Jill and Tony be working with Juanita Arroyo and did it involve murder? Ethan tumbled out, re-entered the car through a rear door and lifted the lid of the terrarium.

"Not so fast, Schwartz."

"My name's Ethan."

"You'd better get your mother's permission first."

He removed the rubber belly and started walking toward the house with it.

"Get back here."

"Why?"

"You know why."

He picked up his pace.

I wasn't about to chase him.

CHAPTER 24

"IT'S NEVER SO BAD THAT IT CAN'T GET WORSE."

-- The Matchmaker's Bible

I jumped on the south 405 and continued toward the Sepulveda Pass. My Bluetooth announced a call. I tapped the switch.

Jill shouted, "How dare you give my son a snake?"

"You've got it all wrong."

"The damn thing just ate my canary."

"I'm so sorry."

"Sorry? You should be sorry."

"He was supposed to ask for your permission."

"What gives you the right to drive my son home from school anyway? You can pick up the snake right now."

Before I turned the car around, I made sure Jill and Ethan were alone.

I returned to Snakes R Us and plunked the terrarium on the counter in front of the man with the handlebar mustache.

"I'd like a refund," I said, fetching the sales slip from my purse.

The salesman lifted the snake out and slid its tail across a bar-code scanner. "Sorry, lady, it's not one of ours."

"What do you mean? You sold it to me. I was here less than an hour ago." I shoved the sales slip at him. "How can you say it's not one of yours?"

"It doesn't have a microchip like ours," he said with an indignant note.

"Do you think I give a damn? You said I could bring it back."

"Looks like one of those raised in China. People are always trying to switch snakes on us, you know."

"C'mon. It even ate for free."

He pursed his lips. "What did it eat?"

"A canary."

"Was it poisonous?" He stroked his mustache.

"Let me speak to the manager."

"I am the manager," he said in an oily voice. He glanced at the rubber belly. "Besides, it looks a little used."

Fuck him. I decided to donate the thing to the West Los Angeles animal shelter. By the time I arrived, the one-story brick building was closed for the day. Let them worry about it. I shoved the rubber belly through the drop box and heard a squawk.

Be still my heart. The canary couldn't possibly be alive inside the rubber belly now. I struggled to get the boa back, but it slipped out of my hands and down the chute. I let go, afraid of joining it.

An androgynous woman stuck her head out the door. "Did you just put a snake down our--"

"I thought you were closed."

"You did, didn't you?"

"Why didn't you answer your door?"

"Of all the nerve...What's your name?"

"What's yours?" I cut out of there, feeling like a murderer.

My heart palpitated. I checked my rearview mirror. What if the cops were to come after me? The terrarium was still on my backseat. I imagined a pair of handcuffs locking around my wrists. That had to have been one of the dumbest moves of my life.

I navigated through Santa Monica to Venice, trying to pull myself together. Revitalization of the canals had led to McMansions and forced out most of the gangbangers. Tchotchke and vintage clothing stores, art studios and ethnic restaurants continued to foster the city's free-spirit charm. A picture of Jill and the bruiser flitted through my noggin. Oh, to be a fly on the porch during their conversation.

What had caused the murders? Given Fong's death in Alexis' bed, semen found in her lifeless body and presence of snakes on each victim, I suspected crimes of passion but wondered what the DNA evidence would show. Also, the missing patent diary struck me as too much of a coincidence to ignore in establishing a motive for the killings. The same was true for Jill's conversation with the bruiser. Fueled by my hunch, I took a chance on finding Tony Hammond at his tattoo parlor. The brochure I'd grabbed at the tattoo convention was still in my purse and I looked up the address.

Less than a block from the boardwalk, popular with tourists because of its carnival atmosphere, the name Sweet Pain of Venice leaped out at me from a storefront. I steered the car into a space next to a

Corinthian column, on which somebody had painted a hula dancer. Hubba, hubba. The early evening air reeked of whiskey from a nearby bar.

I lifted myself out of the car, set the alarm and fed the meter. The waves lashed the shore and a damp sea breeze sprayed my face. I wandered over to the store. A small sign in the window elevated body art to new heights. It said: Things you can't do here: EAT, DRINK, SMOKE, FORNICATE. What about murder? The back of my throat tightened. I thrust open the door and proceeded inside the narrow space slowly. Sample creations covered the walls and a skeleton mobile hung from the ceiling. A rail separated two barbershop chairs from a viewing area. Tony fashioned a design on the arm of a coed type, while a couple of her girlfriends stood watch, giggling. I headed over to him.

"Yo, Tony."

He spun around, ink gun vibrating. "You again?" He turned back to his subject.

She slumped in a chair with her arm extended for the final touches on a butterfly design.

"What's the story with Abu Sayyar?"

"I don't have to talk to you. Get the hell out of here."

"Careful. You might end up chained to an ankle bracelet with a boa wrapped around it."

"You sound like a cop."

"Ex-probation officer."

He said with a shrug, "I'm clean."

"I just left your girlfriend. She wasn't very complimentary."

"She has quite a temper."

"What about yours?"

He did a double take. "What'd the bitch say?"

"You gave her a shiner?"

"That's a lie."

The coed bolted from her chair.

Tony said, "Wait. I'm not finished."

The coed grabbed her friends. "Yes, you are."

Tony followed me out, cursing. "What the hell are you trying to ruin my business for?"

"Somebody attempted to kill me the other night."

"It wasn't me."

A teenage boy with a mohawk haircut flew past us on roller skates.

Tony's hands slid to his hips. "Listen, I may have swindled a couple of people in the past, but I'm no murderer."

A tattooed tower crested along his neck. I zeroed in on the road leading up to it hoping I was on the right path. "Did you ever find Alexis Grand's patent diary?"

"No, did you?" He searched my face as if it might provide crucial information.

"When I saw your girlfriend with that Abu Sayyar creep today, I thought maybe..."

"You thought wrong."

"I'm not here to make trouble for you. I'm just trying to find out why somebody killed two of my clients and tried to--"

"How would I know? I told you, lady, murder's not my style."

I came away from Tony Hammond believing I had more work to do. Although I had no idea what it ought to be, I regarded it as a last ditch effort to make something important happen.

Later that evening, I visited the Queen Mary bar and female impersonation club, hoping Sally's memory had improved. Previous males looking for current ones crowded into the club. Their voices and laughter drowned out strains of "Wait Till You See Her." I cut across the room, keeping an eye out for Sally.

The bartender Teddy wore his usual dour expression, as he mixed drinks at the bar. I wiggled next to a platinum blonde with a hairy back and ordered a glass of merlot.

"Do you come here often?" the platinum blonde asked.

"I'm looking for Sally. Do you know him?"

"Everyone knows Sally."

I gazed past the platinum blonde. "I don't see him."

"You won't tonight."

"Where is he?"

"He's working." The platinum blonde adjusted his bustier. "Check out the corner of Sunset and Genesee, honey, from nine thirty on."

Was Sally hooking as a male or female? If he were in transition, wouldn't his genitals shrivel up? Let's not go there. I wound around Coldwater Canyon to the bright lights of the Sunset Strip. The abundance of clubs, restaurants and billboards dropped off abruptly at Fairfax. I continued east a few more blocks in the darkness to Sunset and Genessee. I slowed down and peered out the window. Where was Sally? The area was desolate, except for a handful of ladies of the night and almost ladies of the night.

My phone gave a holler, which I acknowledged. Zach asked what I was doing. Although I had been keeping my distance from him, I was so glad to hear his voice, I could have kissed him on the nose. I gave him an earful about Sally.

"Where are you?"

"Staking out the corner of Sunset and Genessee."

"Stay there. I'll be right over."

I heard a tap on the window and gasped. A beggar wanted three dollars and fifty cents from me to buy a Starbucks latte. I suggested he try the market down the street, where it was probably cheaper. I made sure my doors were locked, checked my rearview mirror and waited for a sighting.

About fifteen minutes later, the street light illuminated Zach galloping down Genessee. I blew my horn and he waved at me. Several yards away, a Corvette hurtled to a stop, and a beefy person in a sequined number peeled out of the passenger door. The transsexual hobbled to the curb, flashing a pinkie ring like Sally's and stopped beside a street lamp. I rolled down my window and stuck my head out.

"Is that you, Sally?"

Zach hung back.

Sally stepped over to the car, looking wasted. "Do I know you?"

"Alexis' friend, Chloe Love, from the Queen Mary. They told me you'd be here. Aren't you afraid of getting killed?"

"If they come here, they know what they're getting and so do I. Besides, it costs money to transgenderize, more than I'll ever see as a clerk for the city. Hey, I've been meaning to call."

"You remembered the name of Alexis' date?"

Sally poked his head in my passenger-side window, smelling of booze and cheap perfume. "It's the name of a restaurant."

"Which one?"

"It's on the tip of my tongue."

"Think, Sally."

He squinted at me. "Hey, honey, who's your plastic surgeon?"

"The one who did my eyes?"

He snickered. "The one who whacked off your weenie."

I gazed in the mirror and felt my chin, wondering if I needed a shave.

Another john pulled up to solicit Sally's charms."

"Italian, French, Chinese, Japanese?" I shouted out the window.

He gave a shrug and took off with the john.

Zach ambled over to my car.

I opened the door for him and said, "Why didn't you join us?"

"I didn't want to spoil it." He eased inside, smiling. "You seemed to be doing fine without me. So what'd you learn?"

"Can you imagine? Sally thought I was a transsexual."

Chuckling, Zach eased onto the passenger seat. "I'll be glad to set him straight."

"And he tried to remember the name of Alexis' date at the Queen Mary but couldn't think of it."

"Zach caressed my cheek. "Will you have dinner with me tomorrow night?"

Here we go again.

I sprang for a manicure and blow-dry the next morning, then slipped into my final-sale Armani for Nathan's documentary.

He showed up in my office with a spray bottle of something called Gorillas of the Mist.

"What's that?"

"I'm planning to get Jane Goodall involved in my marketing campaign."

A cameraman began to lay cables as a makeup artist, whose lilac eye shadow harmonized with her violet eyes, sat me down in a chair and wiped my face with a wet sponge.

Nathan asked, "Do you have any other props that might work?"

I called his attention to *The Matchmaker's Bible* on my reference shelf.

"I'm looking for something more visual," he said with a gimlet eye.

"What about this?" I directed him to my photo gallery of clients.

He pursed his lips. "Don't you have any credentials or diplomas?"

"Nothing that speaks to gorilla mating."

Garcia and Lyons stumbled into the lobby, dodging cables on the floor.

Lyons looked down at his feet. "What's going on in here?"

I briefed him about the documentary.

"Sorry to disturb you," he said. "Do you know a man named Salvatore Carmona?"

"I don't think so."

"He also goes by Sal or Sally."

I jerked away from the makeup artist's grasp. "Sally?" I paused a moment. "I know a Sally."

"We thought you might."

"What's up?"

"We found him in an alley with a snake around his neck."

My eye began to twitch. I turned to Nathan. "I'm sorry. You'll have to come back."

He said in a cavalier tone, "That's all right. I've got backup. My sister once did a Charmin commercial."

"What about my six thousand clams?"

"Guess not."

CHAPTER 25

"MATCHMAKER, MATCHMAKER, MAKE ME A CLIENT."

-- The Matchmaker's Bible

Nathan and his crew rolled up cables and wheeled out cameras while conversing with each other in loud voices.

"What were you doing with Sally the other night?" Lyons asked above the din.

"What makes you think I was with Sally?"

"We received an anonymous tip."

"I was trying to find out who Snake Man is."

"And did you?"

"No, as it turned out."

We ducked as a woman carrying a bank of lights almost collided with us.

Lyons resumed his questioning. "Did Sally appear to be worried about anything?"

"Not that I could tell."

"Who else was around at the time?"

"Some other hookers, a panhandler, Sally's john."

"Did you get a license plate?"

"It was dark. I was with a friend."

"A friend?"

"My friend Zach Hoffman." I volunteered his phone numbers, relying on him to vouch for me.

I gazed out the window, still reeling from the news of Sally's death. What had the snitch told the cops? Why did he try to frame me for Sally's murder? A strangler got off on strangling people. First Fong, then Alexis and her dog. Now Sally. I disliked being toyed with like a cocktail straw. I heard my landline and screened the call. Nila, the psychic across the street, identified herself in a reedy voice. Although I had never met the woman and lacked the spiritual gene, I picked up the receiver.

"What is it Nila?"

She hesitated. "I can't discuss it over the phone."

"If you're trying to drum up business, I'm not interested." I hung up and sat down again.

She called back.

"Do you know how much my rent is? My rent's twenty-three hundred dollars a month. Do you know what percent comes from my clients?"

"I don't care. Our cosmic worlds are different, Nila. You've got the wrong person. Thanks anyway." I replaced the receiver.

She wouldn't quit. I grabbed my handset. "Nila, will you stop bothering me?"

"I had a dream last night. A person close to you is dangerous. He's going to harm you. So are you ready for a little information exchange yet?"

I entered Nila's psychic parlor, pushed back its beaded curtains and recoiled from the smell of incense. Nila was a woman with a mole on her nose as big as a pencil eraser. She greeted me with excitement and dragged me past a mobile of stars, sun and moon to a table next to a magazine rack that contained *The Bloomberg Report*. I glanced at the price list on the wall.

"How much is this going to cost me?"

"I wouldn't mind a referral."

"Is that all?"

She gestured to a table in the middle of the hodge-podge. "Sit."

I lowered my body into a chair across from her, unable to take my eyes off her mole. "Tell me more about this person in your dream."

"He's interested in moola. You mustn't get in his way." The artificial light bounced off her crystal ball, to the split ends of her mouse-colored hair.

"What's his name?"

"I don't know.

"What's he look like?"

"I can't tell you."

"What did he say to you? Did he mention anything about a diary?"

"This a book with some pages missing. You'd better be careful. He's going to kill you." She studied her crystal ball. "And he said to wash and wear with the same colors."

"C'mon, Nila."

"And drip dry."

"Give me a break."

"I see a single man in his fifties."

"Yes?"

"Now I'm losing the image. Wait. Now I'm getting it back. Ach, men are something else."

Nila was something else.

She seized my hand. "So who do you have for me?"

"For *you?*"

"Who do you think?" She wrinkled her nose, moving the mole up and down.

"Nila, how's a gifted diviner like you unable to find her own men?"

She said in disgust, "My gifts don't include personal use."

I met Zach in the parking lot of Amici's Trattoria during his dinner break. He smiled and I smiled back. A seductive aroma of Italian cooking stoked my appetite. I tooled over to him and he swaddled me in his arms, kicking up my pheromones. I allowed myself to linger in his embrace and scooped him on Nila's premonition.

He loosened his grip on me, "Think there's anything to it?"

I lifted a shoulder. "She was awfully convincing until she came up with the part about the dirty clothes and her wanting to meet a man."

He laughed. "I'm single."

"Well?"

"No, thanks." He squeezed my arm. "You're enough for me."

My belly churned. I wasn't sure where this was going but felt myself succumbing to the journey. I threaded my fingers through his and strolled into the restaurant with him. The neighborhood Italian joint had a New York flavor. It was empty, so we had our pick of tables. I selected a chair facing the door and studied the menu.

Unable to decide between the chicken cacciatore and baked whitefish with pistachio crust, I glanced at Zach and mentioned the snitch's call. "Did the cops get hold of you?"

"They did. That's too bad about Sally."

"I wonder if his john was the one who killed him and made that call to the police. Too bad I wasn't paying much attention to Sally's john at the time."

Zach informed me he wasn't either.

I mentioned the beggar who hit me up for a latte and said, "I doubt he stuck around after he failed to score some chump change from me." I paused. "Maybe the bartender at the Queen Mary knows something."

"You mean Teddy?"

I nodded. "Don't bartenders usually have an inside track on things?" I invited Zach to join me there after he closed up shop.

I arrived at the club before Zach. Multi-colored laser beams rained on the clientele gyrating on the dance floor to the strains of "Isn't She Lovely." I strode over to Teddy, ordered a drink from him and brought up Sally.

"How well did you know him, Teddy?"

He screwed up his face as though he were sucking on a lemon. "That jerk-off?"

"What's a guy like you working in a place like this for?"

A hint of a smile played on his mouth. "At least I don't have to worry about somebody banging me over the head with a beer bottle. The only fights here take place in front of the bathroom mirror."

I munched on a handful of peanuts and licked the salt off my upper lip. One of the female impersonators rushed over to the bar and requested an apple martini to steady his nerves. He engaged in an intriguing dance step. I asked Teddy what it was called.

"Haven't you heard of the Capote Bounce?"

"I can't say that I have." I took a sip of my merlot, which tasted on the fruity side. "Do you remember seeing Alexis in here with a guy in a snake costume?"

He said with a dismissive air, "I'm so busy pouring drinks and collecting money, I couldn't tell you if there's a marching band running through here at night."

"According to Sally--"

"People are so gossipy."

I felt a tap on the shoulder, twisted around and came face to face with Lyons and Garcia.

"You're just having a drink, I suppose," Lyons said.

"That's right."

He took a step toward me. "We didn't start with the LAPD, you know."

Garcia nodded.

"We started in New Orleans."

"If we catch you getting in our way again, you can forget the cameras, because somebody's going to build over your corpse."

"How am I getting in your way?"

"It's for your own safety."

"Okay."

He waved a finger at me. "Not okay. Okay, Sergeant Lyons."

"I'm leaving."

"And another thing I meant to tell you--"

"I'm leaving now."

I punched in Zach's number and caught up with him before he left the bookstore. "Save your energy. We might as well go somewhere else." I told him what happened.

"Did you speak to Teddy?"

"He didn't know anything, unless he's a good liar." I paused. "I'm considering lying low for a couple of days, getting out of town somewhere to clear my head."

"Hey, I've got the perfect hideaway. I just closed escrow on some property in Ojai."

Ojai, a small town less than an hour and a half from L.A. by car, was a world away from the big city's headaches and traffic.

"You bought a place in Ojai? I thought you were worried about losing the bookstore."

"You'd be surprised what an original *Lord of the Rings* is worth. Okay, maybe a couple of them."

"Have you been holding out on me, Zach?"

He chuckled.

"Actually, I was planning to drive up the coast with Sweet Pea and stop at one of those out-of-the-way motels."

"Why would you want to do that when you can have a whole house to yourself and it's free? Nobody'll bother you there." He added, "Except me."

I felt a little flutter.

"We can take walks, play golf, hang out with the dog. You can even have your own room. I promise nothing will happen, unless you want it to. What do you say?"

The invitation intrigued me. Zach's thoughtfulness, caring and persistence had certainly shaken my dedication to the celibate life. I was out of practice, hadn't been with anyone in years. He was certainly a good kisser. How could I accept an invitation to go away with a man I hadn't been intimate with yet? I'd never advocate it for a client. Wait. He was my client. There was so much about him I still didn't know. Like implosion, it would either blow us apart or bring us together. Push me, pull me, it sounded like the beginning of a country western song.

What about Sweet Pea? She had the capacity to be a wrecking ball. Because of her I had been kicked out of more than one motel. I wasn't about to take a chance on her demolishing Zach's new home. Besides, Ojai was in the country. There were coyotes in the country. I contemplated leaving her with Larry, although it might be tricky, given his opposition to Zach. Before driving out of the lot, I reached for my phone.

Larry answered with a gruff, "What?"

"What do you mean, 'what'?"

I could hear a *Cagey and Lacey* rerun in the background.

"Sorry to disturb you."

"Hey, did you ever see the LSD surfer one? They wait for the dealer to ride in on a wave and bust him. I love it. I just love it."

"Are you going to be around this weekend?"

"Yeah. Why?"

I hesitated. "I'm thinking about getting away."

"Without the dog?"

"Maybe."

"Don't tell me you're going to be with that goomba. What's his name?"

"Watch your language."

"So help me, I don't understand where your head is, Chloe."

A couple of noisy drunks staggered through the alley.

"Okay, forget I called."

"Just a minute. Where's he taking you?"

"None of your business."

"That's a matter of opinion."

"You have my cell phone number."

"Your life's one thing. Sweet Pea's is another."

"Does that mean yes?"

"Believe me, it has nothing to do with you."

CHAPTER 26

"A CLOSED MOUTH GATHERS NO TOES."

-- The Matchmaker's Bible

The next morning, I picked up a chicken Caesar salad for lunch from the supermarket. Several doors down, I spotted a Victoria's Secret. I zipped inside and purchased a pale blue nightie, not too sheer for my gravity-challenged state, but lacy enough to flatter an old broad. Never mind I couldn't afford it. I wanted it. I splurged on a push-up bra and three pairs of bikini panties. It felt good to be in lust again. Before I left the parking lot, I called Zach and accepted his invitation.

Later, I skulked into the office with my purchases, locked the door and changed into my new nightie. I thrust open the closet and began to dance in front of the mirror, shaking my booty and humming Marvin Gaye's "Sexual Healing". At the sound of my landline, I snapped to attention. I leaped for the headset, stubbing my toe on my desk.

"Chloe Love here," I said in a professional voice.

A telemarketer attempted to sell me life insurance. I could use some these days. My call waiting put an end to the conversation.

Zach said, "Guess who the IRS is after."

"Don't tell me." I rubbed my toe with my free hand.

"I have to meet with the accountant on Saturday morning."

Lordy, he couldn't cancel on me. He wouldn't dare. I had too much invested. Was this how the murderer felt? I doubted he'd lost it over some lingerie.

I let go of my foot. "What about Ojai?"

"It just means a later start."

"Books, books, books," I said with a relieved lilt in my voice.

I woke up on Saturday morning with a zit on my chin. Holy Christ. It was a corker. I triaged with Vitamin E and makeup. At least it wasn't a bad hair day. I searched for something to wear. My sexy new push-up bra turned out to be a disaster under T-shirts. I finally settled for a white-eyelet blouse that showed a bit of cleavage to go with my jeans. I heard somebody at the door and looked at my watch. It was only nine a.m. Zach had an appointment with his accountant. My breath caught. What if it wasn't him? I bolted to the window and peeked through the shutters. A thatch of yellow hair protruded above the patio gate. Zach didn't have yellow hair. The patio gate blocked the rest of the person. I trundled downstairs with my BlackBerry, in the event of more trouble ahead.

"UPS," said a crisp female voice.

"Who's it from?"

"Pacific Golf Shop."

"I didn't order anything."

"Are you Chloe Love?"

I instructed her to hurl the package over the wall.

The box was long and narrow, like a snake. Yikes. Wrong store. I lifted it up and shook it. It felt bulky but not heavy. I dragged it into the house, grabbed a kitchen knife and sawed through the packing tape. I flipped back the cardboard sides and brushed aside the Styrofoam pieces. Holy Buddha. A TaylorMade driver. I tore open the card and read:

Now we're twins.
Happy hole in one.
Zach

The present was certainly an improvement over boas.

I rounded up Sweet Pea and delivered her to Larry.

"Tell me something," he said on his porch, above the hum of his electric razor. "Am I allowed to ask what time you'll be home?"

"You're allowed to ask."

"Just so you know, I have a raw-dining class on Sunday at five thirty."

My stomach lurched at the thought of uncooked lumps of soy. Baked, grilled or fried, but raw?

"I understand there's natural estrogen in soy. You'd better be careful. You never know. You might grow boobs."

He shut off his razor. "Don't act pissy." He heaved a sigh. "So is this serious? I mean, is this going to be an ongoing thing?"

Was it lust or Mr. Right? I wondered myself.

"Tofu, Larry."

"Tofu, you."

I rushed home to pack my cosmetics. Before I went up-stairs, I decided to fix some lunch. I removed a bowl of leftover noodles and cottage cheese from the top shelf of my refrigerator and nuked it in the micro-wave. The one concession I made to raw dining was a soft tomato which wouldn't survive the weekend. The oven clock indicated ten after one. Zach ought to be here in twenty minutes. I parked myself in front of the TV with my food and bit into a spicy peppercorn. Michelle Wei took the US Women's Open with a win-ning putt. Did she own a TaylorMade driver? I could hardly wait to tee off with mine. I changed stations and landed on a *Criminal Minds* episode. What triggered a person to cross the line? No lion, tiger or bear would kill more than it needed to eat or defend itself. Only human beings hunted for sport. Who was this Snake Man? Had he ever been in his right mind? I shut off the TV and washed my bowl, plate and fork. The hunk from Homeland Security had told me to notify him, if I decided to leave town. Screw it. I wasn't about to give him or Larry an opportunity to spoil the weekend. Time to brush my pearly whites. I shot into the master bathroom, examined my reflection in the mirror and added another layer of concealer to my zit. My buzzer sounded. I zipped up my suitcase and sprinted down-stairs with it.

I led Zach inside and gestured to my golf clubs, situated next to my overnight case at the door. "You shouldn't have."

"Says who?"

I laughed. "Okay, maybe you should have." I thanked him for my new driver.

He eyed me with an approving glance. "Don't you look lovely?" He cupped my face in his hands and kissed me on the lips softly, then gazed past me with a distracted expression. "Where's Sweet Pea?"

"She's not coming."

"Why?" he said in a disappointed voice. "It's not that kind of place, you know. Besides, I love dogs. Is she with your ex?"

I nodded.

"Tell me something. Is it *really* over between you two?"

I assured Zach it was.

He studied my face. "Does he know about us?"

"This is our little secret," I fibbed. "I haven't mentioned it to anyone."

He sighed. "Let's make a pact we won't mention anything about perps, vics or cops over the weekend."

I gave him the high-five sign.

We piled into his PT Cruiser on a mild L.A. afternoon.

Before he started the engine, he slipped in one of his CDs and pressed Play. "This ought to put you in the mood for Ojai."

I peered at him over my sunglasses. "Cello music?"

"Electric cello music, inspired by elephants."

"In Ojai?"

He laughed. "The composer's from somewhere else."

I restored my shades to the bridge of my nose. At the risk of insulting his musical taste, I said, "It sounds more like a funeral procession." I gave his shoulder an affectionate squeeze.

An expression passed across his profile that I couldn't label. He shifted into gear, lurched from the curb and maneuvered to Pacific Coast Highway. The ocean air smelled like a mixture of dead fish and birds. I hesitated to think of what else lurked on the shore from the polluted waters. A lone sailboat glided along the waves. It looked idyllic but was probably better from a distance, like an oil painting.

We jettisoned past the Carbon Beach estates, trendy shops and Pepperdine University which fronted the Pacific like an upscale beach club. A banner undulated over one of the buildings, bearing the words SHAME ON PEPPERDINE. Shame on Pepperdine for high tuition? Shame on Pepperdine for low wages?

Zach turned inland at Oxnard, giving rise to farm-land. A Spanish radio station blasted us from the car next to us. Zach continued to Ventura, where he picked up Highway 33, the cutoff for Ojai. A half hour later, we neared a farmhouse that featured fresh produce and apple cider.

He slowed down. "Do you mind if we stop? I thought we'd eat in tonight."

I imagined myself at the table in my sexy new nightie. "Mind? Why would I mind?"

He hung a right into the lot and came to a stop next to a lone truck. Arm in arm, we strolled into the crowded market. We ambled over to a table offering cold apple cider. I helped myself to a cup, which left a sweet aftertaste. He grabbed a basket and tossed in a head of lettuce. I added a box of strawberries and couple of ears of corn, the fresh fragrance of which wafted past my nostrils. I couldn't remember feeling as alive and complete.

We returned to the car with our bag of fruit and veggies. Zach let me in, started the motor and rolled across the asphalt parking lot. He hung a right onto the highway. I reached over and stroked his cheek. An invigorating breeze laced through my hair. Before long, a sign in-dicated the Ojai city limits, a tourist spot and home to artists, actors and health enthusiasts drawn to its spiritual charm. Zach cut over to a lane sprinkled with the occasional ranch and horseback rider. We passed a fire warning sign and started up a hill. The air smelled like eucalyptus. On one of the hairpin turns, the car became airborne.

"Take it easy."

"I'm used to it."

"You might be, but I'm not."

My stomach felt queasy. I prayed we wouldn't crash into a bunch of illegals going the opposite way after a day's work in the fields. He turned down a dirt road and continued until we reached a dilapidated house located between a clump of trees on a knoll overlooking a valley of magical light.

Zach killed the motor and said with a beatific smile, "Isn't this the perfect setting for a vineyard? It's going to be called Topa Topa after these beautiful pink mountains."

Was he dreaming? Where on earth would he get the dough for one? I surveyed the dirty siding and attached garage of the house, trying to imagine myself as the lady of the vineyard. His place was more basic than I expected.

"Does it have running water?"

"Only cold."

At least it was off the beaten path and romantic in a rather unspoiled way. In the distance was a construction site. I asked if it was part of his property and learned it wasn't. He was about to acquire a neighbor.

He took my hand and led me out of the car, across a row of pavers to the porch. "Can you just imagine it?" He gestured to a dirt expanse. "This is where I'm going to grow my Pinot Noir and Syrah grapes."

"Do you have enough land?"

"Ten acres."

"More first editions?"

He gave me a mysterious smile.

"This is quite a change for you."

"Not really. My degree was in viticulture. My dream was to become an enologist."

Now that he mentioned it, I remembered seeing a sheepskin from UC Davis behind the bookstore's cash register.

"What about Martians, Mayhem and Magic?"

"I don't need a bookstore. My landlord did me a favor. I can sell my inventory online without any overhead."

We returned to the car to unload.

He discouraged me from bringing in my clubs. "This isn't L.A, you know. You don't have to worry about locking your car."

I looked at him askance.

"Don't worry. They'll be fine."

I rolled in my overnight bag. The house smelled dank. Zach cranked open the old-fashioned windows.

The furnishings consisted of a card table and folding chairs in the dining room, sad-sack couch, pole lamp and TV in the living room and futon in the bedroom.

"One bed?"

"The couch opens up," he said with a provocative look. "If that's what you want."

He was not without wit and charm. After we returned to the living room, he turned on the radio and tuned in a country music station. Billy Ray Cyrus was not exactly my idea of romantic. I told myself not everything had to be an exact match. He offered me a glass of merlot, which I accepted, and he produced a bottle of Silver Oak wine and pair of glasses from the kitchen. Since there was no table, he placed them on the wood floor.

I peered at the bottle, then at him. "That's expensive wine."

"I wanted everything to be perfect for us." He dislodged the cork, poured some wine in a glass and tested it. Satisfied, he filled my goblet. "To us," he said in a toast.

We clinked glasses and sipped.

"Full bodied," he said, holding his wine up to the dying afternoon light with both hands.

Silence.

I surveyed his ponytail spilling out of his baseball cap, sweatshirt and jeans and felt a warm glow. Who could explain chemistry?

Our lips met in a sensual kiss.

"Did anyone ever tell you you're a good kisser?" I put down my glass.

"All the time."

I gave a small laugh. "I'm new at this."

"So am I."

He guided me into the bedroom, to the futon with a navy blue comforter and sheets. He sat down beside me and popped a pill into his mouth. Then, he downed a second one.

"Two?"

"If one doesn't work, the other ought to."

I hoped he wouldn't die on me. He began to caress my breasts and undress me. I helped him with the snaps on my bra.

He mounted me in the darkness.

The lovemaking was awkward at first, not exactly what I pictured. Despite the clumsiness, his touch, stiffy and familiar masculine aroma made me feel like a woman again.

I leaned against him afterward feeling relaxed, content and safe. I studied his face in repose. During my darkest moment, I had fallen in love. Who would have thought it? I smiled. I had needed this to happen. Had I finally gotten it right?

"That was wonderful," he said, rolling over.

I imagined driving a tractor across his vineyard and picking grapes with him. In anticipation, I kissed his shoulder gently.

He began to snore, not just a snore, but a growl. I sat up abruptly, overcome with gloom. Was he just another man who comes on strong, only to disappear into the ether once the conquest is over? I pulled the sheet over me. This was different. I sensed it.

I fetched my bra and panties from the covers and tiptoed out of bed into the bathroom to pee. When I came out, Zach was still sawing wood. I removed my nightie from my overnight, slipped it on and meandered into the living room.

Willie Nelson warbled "Corina, Corina" in his twang. I flicked on the light. Our wineglasses were still where we left them, next to the Silver Oak bottle and corkscrew. I polished off the rest of my merlot and carried the remnants of our cocktail hour into the kitchen. Since the plan was to eat in, I decided to scope the refrigerator. I zoned in on some photos attached to the door with fruit magnets. One depicted Zach teeing off on a golf course. Another captured him in front of the Ojai shack, giving a thumbs-up next to a RE/MAX SOLD sign. A third showed him and another man seated at a bar, wearing party hats and toasting each other with a couple of beers. They looked as if they were having a perfectly good time together. The other man's face was familiar. I was sure I'd seen it before but couldn't place where.

What else did we need for dinner? The corn, lettuce and strawberries could certainly use supplementing. I opened the small freezer compartment of his refrigerator. A package of chicken breasts lay on a shelf next to a quart of vanilla-bean yogurt. Zach had thought of everything. While I waited for Sleeping Beauty to awaken, I took out the chicken to defrost. I closed the refrigerator and focused on the pictures. OMG. Now I remembered where I saw the other man--Fred, the flirty security guard at Neutronics R/D who had let me in with Alexis' badge and gotten himself fired. For a moment, his clothes and surroundings in the pictures had thrown me. How in the hell did he know Zach? Why didn't Zach mention his buddy to me?

Wait. Fred worked at Neutronics R/D around the time Alexis' patent diary disappeared. Zach just closed escrow on ten acres of Ojai land, on which he intended to plant a vineyard. Never mind his first editions story. Could Fred have stolen Alexis' patent diary, unloaded it on terrorists and split the take with his buddy?

The psychic across the street had predicted someone close to me was dangerous and wanted money. Zach was an average-size man with dark brown hair. So he played golf right-handed and once saved me from a snake. His bookstore was only blocks from the Santa Monica main library, from where Snake Man had tweeted, using one of its computers. Was the name of the restaurant on the tip of Sally's tongue Zach's Chop House on La Cienega? It sounded like a good bet now. All of a sudden, I got what was going on here. I held onto the kitchen counter, trying to get my bearings. Jesus, had I just slept with a murderer? I grabbed my purse and tiptoed into the garage to call Larry.

Darkness veiled the garage, except for a thin slice of light from the doorway. I tried to reach Larry on my cell phone. Damn. Thanks to AT&T, I got no signal. Something moved on the floor. A large sack. Then it shifted again. I kneeled next to the sack and attempted to read the packing label in the compromised light. The item originated from *Exotic Animals* and was addressed to Zach. Never mind Tony had ordered a boa from there. It must be a popular place.

CHAPTER 27

"PRACTICE YOUR TEE SHOTS."

-- The Matchmaker's Bible

My head felt like mush. I staggered to my feet and grabbed hold of the wall. I had to get away. Was Zach still asleep? If I were to tap the garage-door release, he might hear me. I couldn't chance it. The other way was through the house.

He loomed in the doorway. "Did you check my garbage, too?" He smiled a disingenuous smile. "I thought this was supposed to be our little secret." He leaped forward and knocked the phone out of my hand.

"Take it easy." I backed away, imagining his fingers on my throat.

"Damn it." He pounded his hand against his palm. "I tried to warn you. You wouldn't listen."

"It's not too late." I felt my lip quiver.

"You could've had all this. For the first time in my life, I had some money in my pocket, thanks to Earth Liberation Front. I did it for you."

"You stole Alexis Grand's diary for me?"

"With the help of my buddy, Fred."

Zach took another step toward me and I retreated further. "Fuck."

He grabbed my shoulders and shook me hard. "You couldn't let it go. You wouldn't stop. We could have been so happy. Now I have to kill you like the others."

A wave of nausea swept through my stomach. "My ex, Detective Larry Chellini, is on his way," I lied. "He ought to be here any moment."

I saw him reach for me and I tried to get away, but everything went black.

My head throbbed. I woke up on a dirt floor in a dark place. I attempted to call for help. Nothing came out of my mouth. Something prevented me from speaking. It tasted like terry cloth. I tried to spit it out, but it didn't budge and I gagged. My hands and feet wouldn't move. I fought against my restraints.

There was something on the opposite wall. Crawl spaces in old houses had grates. I flung my body toward it. Something scratched me--a nail. I couldn't remember the last time I had a tetanus shot. Mildew clung to the air. My head couldn't have been more than three feet from the ceiling. I maneuvered my wrists over the nail, back and forth, back and forth, hoping to loosen the edges of the tape on my hands. I felt the nail puncture my skin but kept working my arms. A piece of binding tore. Whoops. A small furry creature whizzed by me--a rat. Holy friggin' hell. I could hardly breathe. The rat squeaked.

A car rumbled along the dirt road. The noise grew louder and stopped. Headlights illuminated the crawl space, creating a crisscross pattern of a metal grate across from me. The light died. A door slammed. Silence. Zach appeared to have a visitor. I heard footsteps and attempted to yell. The rag muffled my voice. There were other voices. I recognized Larry's. How did he know where I was?

Larry said, "Have you seen Chloe Love?"

"No, I haven't."

"Mmmm."

"What's that noise?"

"Squirrels."

"That doesn't sound like their chit-chit-chit sound."

"Excuse me. Chipmunks."

"Mmmm."

"Maybe I did hear from her, but not for a couple of days."

"I thought she told me she was coming here."

"Mmmmm."

"I'm impressed with your place. Mind if I have a look around?"

Way to go, Larry.

"I'm afraid this isn't a good time. By the way, I wish you'd get that woman off my back. She's been trying to start something with me for weeks. I keep telling her I'm just not interested. It's not very professional of her, you know."

I flung my arms against the nail. A car door opened and closed and an engine started. Please don't go. I advanced toward the grate, feeling an adrenalin surge. Headlights invaded the crawl space again. I heard the sound of tires abrading the dirt road, then footsteps getting closer, which gave way to a scraping noise. The grate fell away. Zach hunched over the crawl space dressed again. He poked his head in and stared at me with a maniacal expression.

"You had to tell him, didn't you? Now I must punish you," he said in a tone molten enough to melt a crayon. "Boas aren't known for their good dispositions, especially when they're hungry." He replaced the grate.

I intensified my efforts on the tape, unwilling to become the snake's dinner. Zach returned with a boa. In the filtered light, it looked white and was about six feet long.

"I picked out something special for you," he said. "An albino with pink eyes."

I didn't care what color it was. Go ahead--kill me. Why bother to drag it out?

He tickled the snake's head. "Go to it, Gorgeous."

I writhed on the floor. Zach released the thing and slid the grate into place. Gorgeous started toward me. Something distracted it--the rat. The snake scarfed it up.

"You weren't supposed to do that, Gorgeous. Now you're going to be sluggish. I guess we'll have to resort to a plan B." He disappeared from sight.

I slammed my hands against the nail. The tape tore again. I continued to rub its edges along the nail and one of my hands broke free. I pulled the tape off the other, then my mouth and feet. Gorgeous watched me as if it were eyeing dessert. My mouth tasted metallic. Could I fit through the grate? I had visions of getting stuck midway and tearing my nightie. The hell with it. I shoved open the passageway with my fists and wiggled through the space. Rip. I got to my feet and hurtled toward Zach's unlocked car in the driveway, scratching my ankles on some weeds. Zach's key wasn't in the ignition. I groped for it under the visor and seat.

He must have taken it with him. I leaned over, grabbed the new TaylorMade driver from my golf bag and started to run with it. The ground was uneven and my foot turned. A fiery stab shot through it. I forced myself to keep moving in the darkness, trying to maintain my balance.

"Where do you think you're going?" shouted Zach.

I peeked over my shoulder. The moonlight shone on him heading toward me.

I raised the club in the air. "Don't come any closer."

Zach gained on me. I pushed through my pain and hobbled to the construction site, where I climbed inside and inched along the rough floorboards of a framed foreman's shack. The air smelled of raw planks. My arms developed goose bumps.

It became quiet, too quiet. A shiver scissored down my spine. I sucked in the air and let it out slowly.

At the sound of footsteps, I grabbed the rail. A sliver of wood snagged my finger. Ouch. I yanked it out and a warm trickle oozed from my pinkie. Blood, my blood, which I wiped on my nightie. I turned around and considered jumping over the rail, but Zach caught up with me. I aimed my club at him. He tore it out of my hand before I connected.

"That wasn't very smart."

He cracked the TaylorMade driver over his knee with such force, one of the pieces--the shaft--boomeranged back at him and struck him in the leg.

"Shit." He grabbed his thigh.

I dove for the club head on the ground. Zach swooped down and stepped on the fingers of my right hand. I felt the circulation cease, heard my knuckles crack. One, two, three, four, five. I screamed. He released the pressure. I got to my feet and he tried to grab me, but I ducked. I seized the club head with my still functioning left hand and ran back outside, behind a clump of trees.

Where was he? I couldn't move my fingers. My dominant hand felt broken. Oh, boy. Oh, boy, oh, boy. Cold air blew through my nightie. I heard heavy breathing and it wasn't mine. I whirled around.

"There you are," he said.

Be still my heart. The leaves above us rustled. I glanced at the tree. A snake undulated along the trunk--brown, unlike Gorgeous. The woods were full of rattlers.

Unaware of the snake, Zach took possession of my neck and pressed on my windpipe. My arms slapped the air. I lost control of the club head and heard it whack the tree. The snake dropped down onto him. He bellowed and his body twitched. The pressure on my throat eased. I stumbled backward, staggered to my feet and struggled to fill my lungs with enough air. The creature had a firm grip on Zach's legs. I swept up the club head, lunged at Zach and smacked him on the temple with it as hard as I could.

His eyes bulged. He grunted and fell to the ground. The snake reared up at me, still wrapped around Zach's legs. I walked away from it, toward Zach's head, waited for it to retreat, then took another swipe at his temple. He lay still, very still. Was he dead? Had I scored a birdie? I didn't stick around to find out.

I hobbled back to the house, clutching my nightie and checking my wake in the moonlight. The snake remained wrapped around Zach. My back felt tight, my hand throbbed, everything hurt. I continued to the house, in search of a working phone. A car came to a halt, flashing red and blue strobe lights in the distance. Some people jumped out with flashlights. I made a feeble attempt to hide my privates, but gave up.

Larry shouted, "Is that you, Chloe?"

"Who do you think it is?"

I limped over to him.

"Cover up." Larry zipped over to me and threw his jacket around my shoulders. "Jesus, you're a mess."

"Where is he?" said a lanky cop next to him, his gun drawn. Based on the man's tan uniform, I guessed Larry had resorted to backup from somewhere in Ventura County.

I gestured toward the clump of trees near the construction site. Another cop with Native American features took off with the lanky one.

Larry said, "What's the matter with your voice?"

"Can't you tell? I'm hoarse."

"Hey, I love it. When we were married, how come you never talked like that?" His lips parted in his signature devilish smile.

"Will you stop?"

"Why? It's a real turn-on. Besides, what's a matchmaker without a sexy voice?"

I surveyed my bloody arms, painful hand, ankle and feet and started to cry.

"Let's get you to the hospital."

"You were right about Zach Hoffman." I pawed the tears on my cheeks. "He killed three people--Fong Arroyo, Alexis Grand and Sally Carmona. How could I be so blindsided? He stole Alexis Grand's patent diary with his buddy, Fred, and unloaded it on the terrorist organization, Earth Liberation Front...I screwed up big time."

Silence.

Larry cuffed me on the chin. "Don't worry. You've still got me."

I studied his face a couple of beats. He did appear to be better and nicer than he used to be.

Another black and white sped into view with its brights on, kicking up a cloud of dust on the unpaved road. Lyons and Garcia jumped out and hurtled toward us with their flashlights, making a crisscross pattern of illumination in the darkness.

"Any snakes?" Garcia said in a cautious tone.

Larry scowled at him. "Is that all you can think of, you big pussy?"

"Take it easy. My wife just left me."

"Poor baby."

I smiled a reassuring smile. "I can help you."

"I'm still married."

I said, "That's okay. Consider it some practice."

THE MATCHMAKER'S TWENTY-NINE COMMANDMENTS

-- The Matchmaker's Bible

1. Beware of the illusion of family. Ditch it and form your own.

2. Resist anything but temptation. Dare to slap your inner matchmaker into submission.

3. A match must take like a vaccination. Pow.

4. A meal is most enjoyable in the company of a soul mate. Find somebody who knows how to cook.

5. A match can be deadly. Stay away from cocktail parties for snakes.

6. Beware of drama queens for clients. The same is true for drama kings.

7. Know your customer. How well do you ever really know anybody?

8. Be careful of felons for clients. Be careful of non-felons for clients.

9. Do as I say, not as I do. Who's perfect?

10. Speak softly and carry a smart phone. Add 911 to speed dial.

11. If you think it's too good to be true, it probably is. When everything's going your way, you're probably in the wrong place.

12. Be careful of second-guessing chemistry. Be careful of second-guessing physics.

13. Trust your intuition. Trust your ingenuity.

14. Be careful of snakes wandering through the grass. Red and yellow kills a fellow. Red and black is a friend of Jack.

15. The pieces must fit like a sectional couch's. Don't try to fake it.

16. A matchmaker can't be shy. If you don't know how to dance, get up and shake your booty.

17. One of these days is like none of these days. Sometimes you're the pigeon and sometimes you're the statue.

18. Marriages are made in matchmaker heaven. Be careful about succumbing to your own romantic propaganda.

19. Every path has a puddle. Keep a pair of boots ready.

20. Sometimes a pizza is more than a pie. Cost-effective.

21. No good deed goes unpunished. It's okay to say no after you've said yes.

22. Love and justice are blind. Proceed by touch.

23. Don't get mad, get even. When your feet hit the floor each morning, let the devil say, "Holy crap, she's up!"

24. It's never so bad that it can't get worse. Abandon texting.

25. Matchmaker, matchmaker make me a client. Poof. There you go.

26. A closed mouth gathers no toes. A closed mouth gathers no fingers.

27. Practice your tee shots. You might land a hole in one.

28. Birthdays rock. The more you have, the longer you live.

29. Warning! Don't buy anymore dollar-seventy-five matchmaker bibles from garage sales.

22785183R00176

Made in the USA
San Bernardino, CA
22 July 2015